A Shot in the Cathedral

Mario Bencastro

Translated by
Susan Giersbach Rascón

Arte Público Press
Houston, Texas
1996

This volume is made possible through grants from the National Endowment for the Arts (a federal agency), the Andrew W. Mellon Foundation, and the Lila Wallace-Reader's Digest Fund.

Recovering the past, creating the future

Arte Público Press
University of Houston
Houston, Texas 77204-2090

Cover illustration and design by Robert Vega

Bencastro, Mario,
    [Disparo en la catedral. English]
    A shot in the cathedral / by Mario Bencastro.
       p.   cm.
    ISBN 1-55885-164-X
    I. Title.
    PQ7539.2.B46D513   1996
    863—dc20   96-16942
                                      CIP

Clarification:

With the exception of the historical setting of El Salvador presented in this novel (July 1979 to March 1980), as well as the homilies of Monsignor Oscar A. Romero, his assassination and funeral, all of the other names, characters, places and incidents have been created by the author or have been used fictitiously. Any similarity to real events, places and persons, living or dead, is purely coincidental.

The author

To
Mirella,
Xiomara
and Sergio.

I believe the world is beautiful,
that poetry, like bread, belongs to all.
And that my veins end not in me
but in the unanimous blood
of those who fight for life,
love,
things,
the countryside and bread,
the poetry of all.

Roque Dalton

A
Shot————
in the
Cathedral

I awaken.

I jump out of bed and touch my body anxiously to make sure that I'm alive, that I'm whole, that I'm not dreaming. These days the mere fact of waking up in the morning is cause for real surprise. Death no longer surprises anyone.

Like yesterday, today too I must convince myself that this truly is a new day full of hope for survival, as I try to put aside the shame I feel when I go to the corner store to ask for breakfast and the newspaper on credit.

From the moment I enter and say "Good morning," the owner of the store knows what I'm there for. She casts her usual reproachful gaze upon me.

"I'm going to have a job soon. I'm not lying to you, Doña Consuelo. It's a matter of days."

And of course she doesn't believe me. Why should she? I've been telling her the same thing for six months!

Her gaze humiliates me. Her silence scorns me. I hang my head. My desperation becomes anger. A thick lump blocks my throat and I am unable to speak. The hunger I have suffered for so many months has turned into ulcers, and causes a sharp pain in my stomach.

"All you people are good for is running up a bill! You owe so much and you never pay anything! I can't afford to keep supporting you!"

"Please, Doña Consuelo, I swear; believe me. I'll pay you every last cent."

"So many people asking for credit are going to leave me broke! And then who the hell will pay for you to stuff yourselves? I'm poor just like all of you. The only difference is I don't spend my time loafing around."

They're the same insults she repeats every day. I just pretend not to hear her. I keep quiet. I put up with her scolding, but my face burns with shame.

Finally she gets tired of talking and sees that I haven't left, that I'm still there near the counter with my mouth open and my eyes sad, like a hungry, stray dog, hoping to be thrown some scraps.

Out of pity, or who knows why, she holds out a dish of boiled beans, a couple of tortillas, and the newspaper. She takes out her book and adds numbers to my bill. I owe her so much that adding a little more makes no difference. Still, I do my best to smile and show her that I appreciate this favor with all my heart.

"God will take you to heaven, Doña Consuelo, for being such a wonderful person."

"Forget the thanks; get a job and pay me!"

I feel a strong urge to throw the bowl of beans at her, to tell her and her filthy store to go to hell, and in that way avenge the many insults I've put up with from her at this same time every day for the past six months. But sometimes hunger is much more important than dignity. I should think about tomorrow's beans. I leave the store embarrassed. The burning in my stomach continues, but the hunger has dissipated.

"PRIEST MACHINE-GUNNED TO DEATH."

The terrible news on the front page of the paper makes me hurry as I return to the boarding house where I live. I look for the classified ads only to find reports of the usual disturbances: robberies; fires; labor strikes; takeovers of embassies and government offices; kidnappings of millionaires and political leaders; protest marches against the government; businesses destroyed by bombs. One communiqué sets out the government's new plans: "To mobilize the security forces in the city and the countryside to stop the violence." Many citizens disappear inexplicably. Cadavers appear every day, left in ravines, rivers, and city streets, disfigured by torture, with at least one bullet hole in their heads. Monsignor Romero denounces the massacres from the pulpit of the Cathedral. He implores that the human and constitutional rights of the people be respected, that the violence stop and that reforms favorable to the poor be established.

A job opening! The pain in my empty stomach pushes me to investigate it. Inside the boarding house there is a telephone. As I dial, I imagine thousands of desperate people like myself calling the same busy number. I try again and again and finally they answer. Without waiting to hear my question, the voice announces that the position has been filled. Job openings in the newspaper are scarce. I see no other one that is even a remote possibility for me.

A strange foreboding tells me not to leave home today. The streets of San Salvador are extremely dangerous. It's so easy to suddenly find yourself in the middle of a shootout between police and demonstrators. It's so easy to end up wounded, or dead.... I'll wait. Who knows, maybe some business in the city will respond today to my employment applications.

The sky has clouded. It starts to rain. I listen to the noise of the raindrops on the window. It's as though someone were knocking insistently. The radio announces that the Sandinistas have won. Somoza has left Nicaragua.

The morning passes and the afternoon brings Simón, the owner of the boarding house, to my door. He comes to collect my rent, four months overdue.

"I'll give you one more week to pay. If you don't, though it hurts me to do it, I'll have to evict you."

"I already have a job and I'm starting work next week. I'll pay everything I owe you with my first paycheck."

"I'm tired of hearing the same story every day. Your words, Rogelio, are like a politician's. Nothing but lies."

I close the door, hoping I won't see him tomorrow. Both of us are slaves to the same circumstances. He has no alternative but to accept my promises. If he throws me out, I'll go away owing him, and the room will be empty for an indefinite time, like the other five rooms he's been unable to rent since the tenants moved out. Both of us have come to understand this situation which has no solution other than to wait for things to work out. He knows I can't pay him, yet he comes to collect every day, maybe only to demonstrate his authority. I act offended; he, angry. A sad game played by poor people.

And so the afternoon passed also, leaving me with a bitter taste of frustration in my mouth. Here, in my room, one more day had challenged me. Another day that I had cursed whenever I met it in the corners of my room, when I opened and closed windows, books and doors, when I turned on the lights and turned off the radio, struggling desperately for the victory of a telephone call that never came.

On this night, like on so many others, I must go to bed with my stomach empty, clinging to the hope that sleep may free me, at least in my dreams, from the hunger and debts I've been unable to reduce even by pawning my wristwatch and the treasured class ring from my high school graduation. My situation has forced me to be idle for an indefinite time. I can't afford any painting supplies. When my desperation allows, I content myself with doing pencil drawings on cardboard from boxes I get at the corner store.

Within the shadow of sleep, I let my mind wander to my past occupations. I sold cars that no one bought because they were too expensive. I taught French, which I don't speak, in a night school that was burned by agitators. I was a chauffeur for a rich man who was kidnapped and never found, and a switchboard operator at a bank that was robbed. Humble tasks that let me live modestly but honestly and, above all, allowed me some money to buy supplies and paint at night and on weekends. I am, as Gauguin said before escaping to Tahiti, a "Sunday painter." But now I'm not even that because, although I have time to paint, I don't have enough money to buy even a cheap brush.

Now everything is different. Difficult. Sometimes I wish I'd never wake up.

WE INTERRUPT THIS PROGRAM TO INFORM THE SALVADORAN PEOPLE THAT PROGRESSIVE MILITARY FORCES HAVE DECLARED A COUP D'ETAT. CONSTITUTIONAL GUARANTEES ARE SUSPENDED AND MARTIAL LAW IS IN EFFECT UNTIL FURTHER NOTICE. STAY TUNED TO RECEIVE MORE DETAILS ON THE COUP!

The news spread immediately through the boarding house, and the tenants, gripped by confusion and fear, began to congregate outside in the yard. Some had been sleeping and came out partially clad; others were interrupted during mealtime and came out carrying plates of food. The radio continued to report the decrees of the new government. The children were running around.

"These kids bug me!" said Simón, visibly upset.

"Your fly, Don Simón!" said Bolaños, the mechanic, pointing.

"Oh, excuse me! The news got me out of bed in such a hurry."

He turned on his heels and, with his back to the teacher, zipped up his khaki-colored pants. She, meanwhile, trying to ignore the landlord's indiscretion, was commenting on the innocence of the children who were entertaining themselves playing war. Tenants were coming in and out of their rooms. Conversations struggled to be heard over the shouts on the radio.

"A TRULY DEMOCRATIC GOVERNMENT WILL BE FORMED!"

Bolaños had just gotten home from work and, ignoring his wife's reprimands, took advantage of the confusion and opened a bottle of brandy.

"Let us proudly salute our fatherland! Graduate," he called to Rogelio, "come, have a drink. Don't let me down. How about it?"

"THE HUMAN AND CONSTITUTIONAL RIGHTS OF THE PEOPLE WILL BE GUARANTEED!"

"Graduate, what do you think of it, a new government!" exclaimed Beto, the accountant, who lived in the room next to Rogelio's.

Lupe was making tortillas and heating up beans. Ramona was offering cheese and coffee.

"Come on, let's eat!" invited Simón's wife.

"A TRUE AGRARIAN REFORM WILL BE ESTAB-LISHED!"

"Listen, what promises!" insisted the accountant, truly excited. "Now things are going to change for sure."

The tenants moved around the yard like nervous ants.

"Here are some tortillas," said Lupe.

"Help yourselves to beans and cheese," added Ramona.

"How about a drink?" insisted Bolaños. "Now El Salvador will be straightened out for sure. Cheers!"

"FREE ELECTIONS WILL BE HELD!"

For Rogelio, this day brought something very positive: food. Something especially positive since today he had decided to fast in order to avoid having to beg at the corner store.

"More beans?" Ramona offered Rogelio.

"Yes, please," he answered, holding out his plate.

"More tortillas? And cheese?"

"Yes, thank you."

"AMNESTY WILL BE GIVEN TO ALL POLITICAL PRISONERS!"

"Who wants coffee?"

"Give me another shot," said Bolaños. "After all, coffee doesn't make you drunk."

"HUMAN RIGHTS ABUSES WILL BE INVESTIGAT-ED!"

Noontime found the inhabitants of the boarding house conversing happily beneath the shade tree in the center of the yard. The radio stations broadcast the usual commercials and popular songs, interrupting the programming from time to time in order to inform the public of the latest news about the peaceful coup.

"Come on, Rogelio, sit down!" urged Simón, bottle in hand, content and agreeable. "Let's celebrate the new government. What can I serve you, beer or Tic-tac? Sit down, man; don't be shy."

"The coup happened so fast," said Rogelio, sitting down next to the teacher. "We Salvadorans don't waste time."

"Oh, excuse me!" Simón apologized for having burped. He covered his mouth with one hand and with the other pounded his chest, burping again, unable to control it.

"Oh, come on, Simón, show some respect!" exclaimed his wife. "You act like a horse."

Again the teacher pretended not to notice Simón's imprudent behavior. The mechanic let out a loud laugh and took another drink from his glass of brandy.

"And why not celebrate?" said the teacher, forcing a smile. "Let's take advantage of the occasion; after all, we don't know if we'll live to see another day."

"Good idea!" agreed Bolaños.

"Cheers, companions in misfortune!" shouted Simoncito, a university student and son of the landlord.

"Cheers!" they chorused, raising bottles and glasses.

"This is the time when the deposed ministers are bawling," commented the mechanic's wife, holding a child in her arms. "But we've got nothing to lose; we're just as poor as we were before."

"We gain absolutely nothing," declared the student. "This coup has nothing to do with the needs of the people."

Bolaños offered a drink to the teacher and she took it.

"That's it, Miss!" he said, raising his glass to hers. "Cheers!"

"I prefer a moderate government to an extremist one," remarked the accountant after taking a long drink of his beer. "And it seems to me that that's the way we're going. You see, they're going to free the political prisoners, and permit civilians to participate in the Government Junta. What more do you want?"

"Those are just empty promises," said the student, going toward the table which held the drinks.

The children ran and shouted, hiding among the tenants.

"I killed you already; lie down on the ground!"

"No, you get down; I got you first!"

"I'm a soldier!"

"I'm a guerrilla!"

"My gun is bigger than yours!"

"But I have a tank and you don't!"

"These kids are great," commented Rogelio, as Bolaños put a glass of brandy in his hand.

"Come on, Graduate! Don't fall behind! Bottoms up!"

"Everything is so confusing," said the teacher, straightening her long, black hair. "I don't know what to think anymore."

The student raised his voice, as if he were preaching.

"What is best at this point is decisive action! A profound change to reform the political and economic sectors! To eliminate social differences! A total reorganization!"

"Another drink, Miss?"

"Yes, thank you."

"Of course, this type of change goes beyond personal and class ambitions. It is an action in which individual interests are subordinated in favor of a solution which benefits the majority!"

"That's right!" said Bolaños, staggering. "Down the hatch!"

"Those who have too much must give part of their property to the common good! Power will be shared also!"

"Miss, another little drink? Don Simón? Ma'am? Graduate? Straight or with lemon?"

"In short, work together for our common destiny! And that's nothing new. It's exactly what Jesus Christ tried to do!"

"And what it got him was death on a cross!" remarked Bolaños, gripping his bottle.

"So, ladies and gentlemen, let's just get drunk!" shouted the accountant.

Bolaños continued serving brandy and the student poured beer. The teacher smiled and the accountant kept taking long drinks.

Hours passed as they consumed bottles of liquor and had political arguments representing all positions. The women cleaned off the tables and then served steaming plates of food.

"Cheese, Rogelio?"

"Yes, please."

"Just give me beans and a stiff tortilla," said the mechanic. "I have a poor man's tastes, and I'm not ashamed of it."

In one corner of the yard the student and the accountant had entered into an angry discussion. Beer in hand and with heated arguments, they were arranging and rearranging the country. Several people surrounded them, listening with interest.

"Another drink?"

"Yes, please, thank you."

"More cheese?"

"Very well, thanks." Rogelio went over to where the tortillas were and took three. "You're very kind, Ma'am."

"This graduate sure eats heartily," remarked Bolaños.

"He works like a sick person but eats like a healthy one," remarked Simón with his usual sarcasm.

Then, noticing that night had fallen, they turned on the yard lights. A phonograph appeared. The invitation "Let's all dance!" was heard. Simón and his wife started the dance. With synchronized steps they followed the frenetic rhythm of Paquito Palavicini's song: "El Salvador is a tiny, tiny, tiny,

tiny country; but the other one is a huge, huge, huge, huge one."

The teacher, unexpectedly, grabbed Rogelio's hand and invited him to dance.

"I don't dance, Miss, forgive me."

"Don't worry; the drinks you've had will teach you."

"Pardon me, Ma'am, did I step on your foot? Excuse me, it's the drinks."

"It's your big feet, Bolañitos."

"It wasn't me, Ma'am; the graduate is more drunk than I am."

The yard was converted into a happy dance floor. "Tiny, tiny, tiny, tiny..."

"The country is collapsing and here we are enjoying life as if nothing were happening." Rogelio tried to follow the teacher's lead as they danced.

"We have to take advantage of these rare moments of happiness as much as we can," she said, smiling and moving her hips to the rhythm of the music, moving her body closer to Rogelio's. "Besides, the student and the accountant will find a solution soon, don't you think?" She laughed mischievously and held him closer, treating him with an intimacy he had not offered but was glad she had.

"You're completely right," he said, excited by the drinks and the music, and by the closeness of the teacher's soft, sweet-smelling body.

"I've noticed that you never mix with the rest of the tenants. Why so unsociable?"

"It's just the way I am. I don't talk much. I read and paint. That's all. It's hard for me to make friends."

"Call me Lourdes and I'll call you Rogelio," she said with a smile that made the young man's heart pound. "Okay?"

"Okay," he agreed, containing a sudden impulse to caress her long, smooth, black hair. He felt very excited. He realized that, even though he had never danced before, his legs now moved freely to the beat of the music.

Everyone in the boarding house was dancing, drinking, talking, singing, shouting. Rogelio found all the euphoria very pleasant. Unfortunately, he suddenly remembered that this was only a rare parenthesis in his situation of hunger and anguish, in a chaotic present that forecast a perhaps even worse future. And now, surrounded by sweaty, dancing, noisy, drunken people, facing the delicate body of a woman, intoxicated by the drinks, the laughter, and the music, and with his stomach full, Rogelio felt himself possessed by something so strange that he suspected he was experiencing true happiness, or something like it.

"I am Rogelio!" he shouted suddenly, carried away by a strong impetus of euphoria. "A person of flesh and blood!"

"Hallelujah!" seconded the mechanic.

"May the ugly ones die!" shouted the accountant.

"Long live Monsignor Romero!" exclaimed the teacher.

And everyone responded in unison, "Long may he live!"

Then someone commented that it was after midnight, and Simón's wife turned down the music. Some couples continued dancing soft boleros. With his wife's help, Simón entered his room. The sound of vomiting was heard from the bathroom.

Rogelio was so drunk he could hardly stand. The few steps he had to take to go back to his room represented a great accomplishment. Finally he entered the room, walking in the darkness, and when he felt his knees touch the edge of the bed, he let himself fall heavily onto it. He heard the very distant voices of the Los Panchos' trio singing "without love the soul dies desolate, sacrificed in pain, sacrificed without reason; without love there is no salvation..."

When he opened his eyes, the morning sun was filtering in through the holes around the door and illuminating the inside of the room and, to his great surprise, the face of Lourdes, who was sleeping next to him.

There was a knock on the door. It was Simón. Rubbing my eyes, I waited for his usual threats.

"Are you still sleeping? Quit being so lazy, man! If I were in your shoes I'd be up early every day, going up and down the street to every store and factory, and I bet I'd get some kind of job, even if just sweeping parks."

I thought of telling him that the parks were not swept anymore, that they had become cemeteries, but I stopped myself.

"I can see you just don't like to work. You're one of those people who like to lie around in the shade. Here, this special-delivery letter from *The Tribune* just came for you. Who knows, maybe you'll get a chance to be a reporter, get rich, and forget all about us."

Ignoring the old man's sarcasm, I took the envelope and ripped it open anxiously. "Please present yourself at our offices. Position open." I read it two, three times, still not daring to believe the message. I showed the paper to Simón who read it and let out a laugh.

"What a joke! I thought you'd never get a job, because the only thing you've done in all this time is lie in bed snoring all day. That is, when you haven't been painting those horrible pictures."

The white shirt and black pants, my change of clothes for special occasions, "for laughing and crying," had waited so patiently, hanging in a corner of my room, covered with dust and cobwebs. Now at last I could shake the dust from them and let them give shape to my skeleton, take it out and push it to wait for the bus that goes downtown, guide it to a gray building, put it in the elevator, get it out on the fifth floor making it cough and sweat, and present the letter to the secretary.

"Have a seat in the waiting room, please. The administrator is in a meeting right now. Help yourself to some coffee if you like."

"Thank you, Miss; you're very kind."

My nervous body went toward the waiting room, and as soon as I sat down on the sofa, I stood up again. Hot coffee. Anxiety. Indecisive steps. Examination of the room. One window looked out over the city: in the distance, villages on the mountain slopes. The vibrant, yellow sun looked like a huge gold coin, disproportionate against the blue sky, and the voluminous clouds like gigantic milky spheres. Streets crowded with buses, cars, people, smoke, noise. A protest march was coming down the main street. Signs. Shouts. "FREE ELECTIONS! FREEDOM FOR POLITICAL PRISONERS! WE WANT TRUE DEMOCRACY!"

"Villaverde!" someone called from behind me.

"Yes, sir, at your service," I said, automatically extending an unsure hand which the man did not bother to shake.

"I don't have time for explanations. I just came from one meeting and need to go to others. There's a lot to do here. I need an active person who's willing to do anything. To do cleaning and run errands. I see you're a high school graduate. From time to time you'll be assisting the editor. If you're intelligent, you may become a reporter. Well, that's all. If you accept the job, let the secretary know."

He extended his hand for me to shake it. He walked away and I never saw him again. The secretary handed me some forms to fill out.

"Welcome to *The Tribune*. Your personal data. Write legibly, please. Your name is Rogelio?"

"Yes, Miss, at your service."

"The position pays one-hundred-fifty colones every two weeks," she said in a condescending and somewhat arrogant tone.

She knew those were the exact words I needed to hear at that moment, magic words which, in effect, gave me permission to exist, at least minimally. Those words spoke to me of food and of payment of my debts. They returned to me a right: the right to be someone, to be a productive citizen rather than someone forced to be lazy.

Wasting no time, I began work that same morning. I swept and mopped rooms and halls. In the afternoon I picked up and delivered messages from office to office. Finally the clock struck five and all the employees headed out toward the elevators.

"How lucky I am to have a job," I thought, squeezed into the elevator, surrounded by serious, silent faces. The doors opened and the people rushed out into the street, running to get on the bus.

Once outside, walking among the congestion of automobiles, people, and busses, I noticed the Oasis Restaurant sign. The afternoon heat made me thirsty for a beer, which I planned to drink with great pleasure to celebrate my new job.

The place was deserted, which seemed strange to me, since the restaurant was located in the center of the city. The silhouette of the bartender could be seen in a dark corner. I ordered a Pilsener and he immediately brought a bottle and glass which he placed mechanically on the counter.

"Don't take long, please," he said. "I close at six. I don't want to be caught out on the street after dark."

I lit a cigarette and looked over the empty place.

"Don't worry; I understand," I said. "I don't risk being out after dark either."

Suddenly, the fear and distrust of talking with a stranger about the national crisis held back my words, and I ended up saying them secretly to myself: "We all know that in this country darkness is a synonym for kidnappings, arrests, bombings, arson, and assassinations... When day dawns we thank God that we are alive and well. The city and its people have a different face at night."

The man served himself a beer, too.

I put a five-colones bill on the counter. My desire to drink beer and share with the bartender my happiness at having gotten a job after six months of idleness, shame and hunger, had disappeared.

"I'd better get home, too," I said. "It's really not a good idea to be out walking around in the city these days."

"Don't worry, man," he replied. "If you don't get involved in problems, you have no reason to fear."

He took the bill off the counter and, as he got my change, his face forced an expression something like a smile.

"The way things are now, it's very easy to become involved in problems," I said.

He gave a long sigh, and the attempted smile disappeared from his face. I took my change and headed toward the door.

"We'll see you another day."

"God willing. Take care."

"Thanks."

The man followed me to the door and closed it brusquely as soon as I left.

I joined the people congregated on the street corner waiting for the bus. It soon arrived, crowded as it always was at this time of day. Women, elderly people, children, businessmen in suits and ties, women with huge baskets and men with packages were trying to get on it as though it were the last one. I feared missing it myself and, avoiding the driver's eyes, I sneaked in through the back door while others were getting out. The bus filled up, but people were still trying to get on even after it was moving, resuming its noisy march through the smoky, dirty streets of the city.

As I travelled among motionless sweaty bodies, Ignacio's memory assaulted me. The mystery still disturbed me. What had become of him? My gaze passed through the broken windows of the bus and became lost in the sidewalk. That distant moment when I received the news came to life again in my mind. I remember it all so well: there was a knock on the door. The messenger handed me a telegram. I tore open the envelope and found myself reading the gloomy sentence: "Ignacio died yesterday."

That same day, a few hours later, I called his brother on the phone.

"Really, we don't know the cause of his death," he declared. "When I went down to his studio, I found a note in his handwriting saying that he had committed suicide. The odd thing is that his body wasn't there. You know very well how things are here in El Salvador. People disappear day and night, without any kind of explanation. It's best to not even try to investigate. Just stay there in New York and don't worry. And don't even think about coming here. It's not healthy."

The days passed and countless ideas, none of which explained the disappearance of my friend, tormented me. My desperation grew. The thought of his uncertain death obsessed me...my best friend, my brother painter, my companion in unforgettable adventures, erased from the face of the earth. Why? By whom? There had to be an explanation.

That was why, after living in New York for seven years, undocumented like thousands of others, I returned to my country. I searched for Ignacio, tirelessly, everywhere. I asked about him at the headquarters of the Army, the National Guard, and the National Police, at the Treasury Police and the Municipal Police. I visited hospitals and morgues. I even went to the Interior Ministry. The visits were long and complicated. At the Human Rights Commission they had me look through mountains of photographs, in which I could make out absolutely nothing because they showed faces disfigured by torture and bullet wounds. I traveled to all the newspaper offices and even paid for an ad asking for any information about my friend. Everything was useless. Silence was the only response to my questions.

"The day they kill me, may it be with five gunshots, and may I be close to you," sang a passenger's radio. The song competed with the noise in the crowded bus that traveled through the city immersed in its violent everyday activities.

THE JUNTA, COMPOSED OF THREE CIVILIAN AND TWO MILITARY MEMBERS, HAS TAKEN OVER THE GOVERNMENT. THE UNITED STATES IS PROVIDING THE JUNTA WITH $200,000 IN MATERIAL AID TO COMBAT DEMONSTRATIONS, AND WITH SIX MILI-TARY ADVISORS TO TRAIN THE SECURITY FORCES IN ITS USE.

Editor's office. The furnishings consist of just one bookcase and two desks. There are papers scattered everywhere, even on the walls, where photographs of city scenes, pictures of political and cultural celebrities, and calendars with figures of saints and touristic illustrations hang. One door of the room opens on the corridor that leads to the other offices. One window looks out on the city. Inside the room are two people concentrating on their work. The editor, known simply as Domínguez, is a man of 55 years of age, with gray hair, a dark complexion, of slight build, and an inveterate smoker. His assistant, Rogelio Villaverde, is a beginner in the field of journalism.

Domínguez: You sure learn fast, Rogelio. It's amazing that in the short time you've been working here you've learned to copy articles and proofread. I'm very satisfied with your work. I believe you'll soon be ready to go out, collect information, and write your own articles.

Rogelio: Oh, that's not important. Being a reporter seems too complicated to me. I don't think I'm cut out for that.

Domínguez: It's easy. All you have to do is pay attention to current events.

Rogelio: I'm afraid my emotions would get in the way.

Domínguez: Forget your emotions. When you write for a newspaper, you reflect the incidents without exaggerating or including personal opinions. Give the facts as they are and not your own viewpoint. We represent a voice of moderate opposition, with well-measured words.

Rogelio: A calculated game.

Domínguez: That's right. Coldly calculated. Because one must realize that in this country the right wing has, and always has had, control of the press. Although we're a small newspaper with limited circulation, we mustn't become careless and publish something too strong against the government. If we did, that would be the end of everything.

Rogelio: I don't understand how any newspaper, however insignificant it may be, with a viewpoint different from the official one and from those of the other press media, can exist here.

Domínguez: Well, we exist because, among other things, the owner comes from a certain wealthy family, and we are so small that we don't constitute a direct threat to the current regime. But of course the time will come when the situation becomes so difficult that they won't permit even the most minimal opposition. Until that day comes, we operate. You could say that our days are numbered.

Rogelio: Then, you can never tell the truth openly.

Domínguez: Well, I think we tell the truth; what happens is that we're forced to disguise it. But, between the lines we say, for example, that the reforms the Junta proposes are not viable, that they're the same promises as always, that they're only adding the little word "revolutionary" to make them sound better, but that when all is said and done they mean nothing.

Rogelio: And why not say it like that, then?

Domínguez: Because, like I told you, you have to know how to say it. We don't exist just to contradict the government either, but to present an opinion that offers alternatives. That's the function of a progressive and responsible press.

Rogelio (a little upset, returns to his desk): Telling the truth in disguise is the same as telling a lie. In that way, this newspaper is no different from the rest. Now I understand the part about the "coldly calculated game."

Domínguez (following the young man, who still has his back to him): I understand your frustration, Rogelio. I was young once, too. I dreamed of becoming a great reporter. A free thinker. Of denouncing abuses. Of defending the weak. But from the beginning I realized that journalism doesn't exist here. We're nothing more than simple commentators with limited, if not nonexistent, room for action. If we go too far, we run the risk of a dark disappearance. Do you understand the game and its consequences, young man? Do you? (Looking him in the eye.)

Rogelio: It's quite clear.

Domínguez: That's the way I understand it. Nevertheless, I have to tell you that every night I go to bed thinking about all the truths we could have published if we were in a country where true freedom of the press existed. Usually I can't even sleep; my conscience won't let me. Several times I've tried to quit this job but, since I'm used to eating three times a day, I take the coward's way out and opt for the easy alternative of complacence, especially when I think that, in a country like this one, nothing changes anyway.

Rogelio: Maybe what gives meaning to our reporting is that, however insignificant it seems, it represents hope for those who are struggling to change things; it's a minuscule support in solidarity with their aspirations.

Domínguez: Minuscule support in solidarity? What a phrase! Now you're getting into it... That's it, Rogelio; you said it. That's our reason for being... And, getting back to reality, as you know, Villaverde, we're short of reporters. One is sick. Another changed jobs out of fear of the consequences of this one. There are so many things happening in this city and we need to cover them. Therefore, I'm forced to send you to interview the members of the Popular Revolutionary Block who have occupied the Cathedral. You'll be going with Ramos, the photographer. I want you to bring me enough material for this week's edition. (He gives him a card.) Present this *Tribune* identification card so they'll let you enter the church.

Rogelio (objecting to his boss's orders): But, Domínguez, don't you understand that I don't know what to do? I wouldn't know where to start.

Domínguez: Don't worry. Just ask them anything. They'll tell you everything, even what they've had to eat! They love publicity. If they didn't, they wouldn't do these things.

(There is a knock on the door and Ramos comes in, carrying his equipment.)

Domínguez (going forward to greet him): Ah, it's none other than *The Tribune's* great photographer.

Ramos (approaching Rogelio): They tell me we'll be working together. I hope you're prepared for the hard knocks. Look, this is from being hit yesterday during a demonstration. They don't call me Bruise Ramos for nothing.

(Ramos lets out a laugh. Rogelio, shy and quiet, remains in his corner. Domínguez gives Rogelio a pencil and notepad, and then addresses the photographer.)

Domínguez: Hey, Ramos, don't be such a crybaby; you know those things are part of the job. Now go to the Cathedral and don't come back until you've gotten a full report with good pictures. Get going!

(Ramos leaves the office. Rogelio follows him with apparent indifference. Domínguez, meanwhile, has remained standing in the center of the office, observing the ceiling enigmatically.)

One weekend Rogelio and I finally went to Ilobasco, my home-town, which is located in Cabañas, 55 kilometers from San Salvador. My whole family is from there; my grandparents' ancestors inhabited these lands many centuries before the Spaniards arrived. Ilobasco, o Xilobasco, comes from the Ulúa word Xilo-huax-co, which means "In the tender reeds." Ulúa was the second most common indigenous language, after Pipil, in the land now known as El Salvador. My parents carry traces of the ancient and grandiose blood of people who were hard workers, artists, stone and clay artisans, builders of tem-ples and pyramids, poets and warriors, who belonged to the Mayan civilization which extended from Uxmal and Chichén Itzá in Yucatán, México to Tikal, Copán, and Tazumal in Cen-tral America.

I was anxious for my parents to meet Rogelio. I had told them so much about him that they were interested in meeting him, too.

I remember so clearly all the details of the trip, which began one hot Saturday afternoon when we boarded the bus at the eastern terminal.

We got on and took seats in the back. Very few people were traveling. A half-hour later, the vehicle left the station reluctantly, incredibly slowly, and turned onto a cracked and dirty street. The small number of passengers rode in complete silence. Perhaps they were fearful because of the uncertainty of a trip into the interior of the country. Maybe they were uneasy about the bus, which looked as though it might fall apart at any moment.

The monotonous sound of the engine and the desolate countryside invited boredom. I asked Rogelio to tell me about one of his many nightmares, and he did. When he finished, I commented that he could write a story based on the dream.

"I devote all my free time to painting," he said.

My interest was so great that I said I would write it myself. Rogelio didn't know I had that ability and was surprised to find out that I wrote poetry.

"You say it as if it were a simple thing. I'd like to read something of yours. I love poetry. I once tried to write verses, but I realized that to say what I want to I need color and form."

I replied that poetry, in a way, also uses colors and shapes.

"I've written since I was 14 years old. I've never published anything because, besides being difficult, in this country literature is not valued. When you say you're a poet, people look at you as if you were a bum or a crazy person. Worse if you're a woman."

"The same is true of the visual arts. The only reason I paint is because it makes me forget reality. It's my therapy. The rest doesn't matter to me. I'll work at any job to be able to afford to paint. I know perfectly well that my paintings won't feed me. Nor do I hope to influence anyone. Most people are poor. And the fortunes of the rich drown them in indifference. The others, who are just getting by, need to worry about keeping their jobs and surviving."

"Your comments are sad but true, Rogelio. In this country culture is not valued. Art is a luxury to which we poor people can't aspire."

"In this land the artist is nothing! That's the way it is, Lourdes, we're nothing. You because of your pen and I because of my brushes. What a tragedy, don't you think?"

Both of us tried to smile, but I remember that neither his smile nor mine managed to hide our sadness. Sometimes even smiles refuse to be accomplices in our self-deception. The conversation left me with a dark feeling of desolation. Rogelio was pensive and perhaps sad also. I moved closer to him and, holding his hands in mine, whispered a poem to him:

> The little bit of love
> that still surrounds the world
> saves it from total chaos.
> Therefore
> we must shout love,
> bring it out of our dark and lonely depths,
> so that it may act as a furrow
> and germinate the flower
> of a much greater love:
> Love of humanity.
> Love of everyone
> and for everyone.
> Because otherwise
> it is only love of ourselves:
> Despotic love.
> Love of one
> and not of all.

GUERRILLA GROUPS INTENSIFY OFFENSIVE "IN RESPONSE TO REPRESSION BY THE SECURITY FORCES AND THE JUNTA'S INABILITY TO ESTABLISH TRUE REFORMS." SIX PLANES BURNED IN SANTA CRUZ PORTILLO—A COFFEE GROWER AND TWO LEADERS OF THE FAR RIGHT EXECUTED. REBELS RELEASE NINE HOSTAGES, INCLUDING NORTH AMERICAN PEACE CORPS MEMBER.

Domínguez: What an excellent story Rogelio wrote! He has a great future as a reporter.

Rogelio (as if he had been expecting to hear those words, gets up from his chair, irritated): This job is meaningless... Just a few hours ago I interviewed that young man, and I just heard on the radio that his body was found this morning near the Cathedral. What a tragedy! I remember that he spoke to me of his ideals, of his willingness to give his life if necessary so that things would change... Do you understand, Domínguez?

Domínguez: Yes, I understand...

Rogelio (raising his voice): No, Domínguez, forgive me for saying it, but you don't understand! That young man gave his life for us, for his friends and for his enemies... so that this country would be a decent place for everyone. Is it fair that he should die like a dog for wanting to straighten out this world? (He throws some papers on the desk scornfully.) And we are here measuring our words!

Domínguez: No, of course it's not fair. I know it's not. But this is the status of journalism here. Don't let yourself get frustrated! Reality forces us to go on, Rogelio, to get used to blood... to death. Keep writing and do it with the conviction that we support the ideals that will build a better world. It's our only consolation. (He goes toward the corner of the room where, on a small table, there is a jar of instant coffee and a

small pot of water on a hot plate. He fills his cup, lights a cigarette, and returns to his reading.)

Rogelio (bitterly): You may be right, Domínguez. Besides,
this is just a job and we're just common people, laborers. We
have no say in the business. We're here to perpetuate a sad
tradition of empty and anonymous newspaper commentators
writing articles and editorials that never manage to change
the situation.

Domínguez (approaches Rogelio with some papers):
You've said it, Rogelio. That's journalism in this corner of the
world. An exercise in words that has nothing to do with anything. Reality is already determined; it's unchangeable.
(Adopting a paternalistic attitude, a bit melancholy, as if
explaining the bitter reality of things to his own son). I know
very well that disillusion is a hard pill to swallow, especially
when you're young and full of beautiful and healthy ideals.
But don't worry, Rogelio, after work we'll have a few drinks
and you'll see how fast you forget your disappointment.
Drinks are fundamental in this job.

That afternoon after work, the editor and his assistant headed for the Oasis Restaurant. The bartender recognized Domínguez immediately. He greeted them, showed them to a table in the back, and said he would bring them some beer.

Domínguez began to tell, with a certain bitterness, of the effort he was making to keep going in his job at *The Tribune.* He spoke of his lonely life. Although the young man's silence seemed to make him uncomfortable, he did not stop talking; he kept filling the glasses with beer and insisting that Rogelio drink.

"Drink up, drink up; it'll cheer you up."

Several policemen entered the restaurant, and Domínguez immediately stopped talking and observed their movements.

"This smells bad. Something big is going to happen here. Be ready to get down under a table when the action starts, and don't move until it's over."

"Maybe they're just thirsty and came to have a soda."

"I don't know why, but I think they're looking for someone who's here."

At the precise instant that one of the policemen lifted his glass to take a drink, four men sitting at the table near the door drew pistols and shot at the policemen, who immediately returned fire.

The editor and his assistant threw themselves to the floor. The gunshots created panic among the customers, and screams of pain mixed with the noise of breaking glasses and bottles and the crashing of chairs, tables, and bodies. The shooting lasted a few minutes and none of the participants was left alive. The surviving customers came out of their refuge under chairs and tables. Domínguez brushed off his clothes and rushed toward the exit.

"Let's get the hell out of here!" he said, stepping over and around disfigured dead bodies lying in pools of blood, pieces of broken glasses, bottles and plates, spilled food, and pieces of furniture.

Curses and the groans of the wounded could be heard.

"What shitty times! You can't even drink a beer and relax."

Domínguez managed to get out of the building.

"Let's go, Rogelio, hurry! Come on, don't just stand there! If we do, we'll be in a mess."

A taxi stopped and they hurriedly got in. Following Domínguez' instructions, the driver took them through Barrio Modelo, then to Colonia Minerva near the President's home, to take the highway toward Planes de Renderos. Ten minutes later, they left the main road and turned onto a dusty, lonely trail. Rogelio rode in silence, still frightened after the shooting at the Oasis. His boss talked tirelessly about everything, and the driver listened patiently without interrupting him. The car stopped in the midst of a thick grove of trees in front of a house that looked abandoned. The boss paid the taxi driver and they got out.

"What is this? A haunted house?"

"You'll see," said Domínguez, and knocked on the door.

A voice answered: "Who is it? What do you want?"

"Domínguez. Open up."

The door opened, they went in, and the door closed behind them immediately.

The bus slowed down. National Guardsmen were stopping traffic. After a half-hour wait, an officer finally got on the bus and ordered us to get off and line up on the side of the road. A Guardsman approached us and asked to see our identification cards, which made me nervous. Rogelio noticed my discomfort and, to reassure me, began to stroke my hair.

"Don't worry, Lourdes; it's just a routine inspection."

Meanwhile, several Guardsmen were searching the inside of the bus, rummaging through packages and emptying the contents of purses and bags onto the seats.

The agent examined our documents.

"Where are you going? On your honeymoon?"

"We're going to Ilobasco, to visit her parents," answered Rogelio patiently.

"And who is she? Your wife? Your girlfriend? Tell me."

"My girlfriend," said Rogelio. I was biting my lip, now not from nervousness, but from anger.

"What do you do? What kind of work?"

"I...I'm a painter," he said, deciding not to mention that he was an editor at *The Tribune*.

"What kind of painter? A house painter?"

"A painter of paintings," he responded, not knowing what to say.

"Oh, you paint landscapes. An ar-tist," remarked the agent, accenting the syllables mockingly.

"Exactly," affirmed Rogelio without losing his calm.

"Well... I wonder when my painter friend can do my portrait," said the Guardsman, his rudeness suddenly replaced with a friendly attitude. "Do you think you can do a little portrait for me?"

"Yes... Of course... But not right now, another time."

"I'm going to give you my address," he continued, extremely interested in the portrait.

"Well... of course," said Rogelio, feeling obligated to accept the insistent request of the agent. "I'll paint a great portrait for you."

"But don't forget. This is my address in town. My name is Ramón; I'm at your service. Here are your papers. Everything is in order. Have a wonderful honeymoon," he said, winking at us and laughing.

Meanwhile, the other passengers had already gotten on the bus. Rogelio picked up our bags. The driver started the engine and asked us to hurry. When we were getting on, Rogelio felt a hand on his shoulder. He turned around, thinking it was mine. Then he saw the face of the Guardsman, so close to him that he could see the inside of the man's mouth when he talked.

"Listen, my painter friend, be careful and behave yourself. Don't end up like that painter they killed for being a guerrilla."

Confused, and now impatient, Rogelio said he didn't know what the Guardsman was talking about.

"That guy, man. That painter named... Ignacio... Yes, Ignacio... I don't remember his last name. But anyway, be careful; don't go and die on me before you do that portrait. See you."

Rogelio jumped on the bus. The driver closed the door and stepped on the gas. I then noticed on Rogelio's face the stupor that the startling words of the Guardsman had caused.

"Ignacio dead? For being a guerrilla? It can't be," he murmured.

Rogelio was perplexed. He said that, after all, he would go to see the Guardsman the following week.

"I'll paint his picture as an excuse to get information from him about Ignacio."

I looked at the long line of paralyzed vehicles. I imagined the frustration and weariness on the travelers' faces as the authorities examined their papers.

"What a waste of time," I said, exasperated at the delay.

"Don't get upset over such an insignificant thing," begged Rogelio. "At least it wasn't any worse. Besides, it's not their fault; it's their job. They're only following their commander's orders. The members of the National Guard are just ordinary people, like you and me, who have to work hard to earn their daily bread, too."

"I understand, but many of them carry their duties to unnecessary extremes."

"Forget it, Lourdes. Let's talk about something else. Why don't you read me another one of your poems? I liked the last one a lot. I want to hear more of your poetry. We still have almost an hour to go."

"Let's see what you think of this one," I said, taking a paper out of my purse and reading it to him:

> No matter when, how, or where,
> the time will come
> to answer for so many deaths.
> The spilled blood will nourish
> the bones of a child.
> That child who will wonder
> why he was born without a father,
> why he grew up without a mother,
> why his innocence was stolen.
> That child who tomorrow will be a man
> and will demand an accounting.

"Hi, old man," said a woman with bright red cheeks, blue eyebrows, purple lips, and false eyelashes.

"How's it going, Gorda?"

"And who's this boy with the saintly face?"

"He's a young reporter with a great future." The boss hugged the woman. "I want you to get him a good girl, so he can forget about a little scare he just had."

"Well, come on in! We're all first class here. Starting right here," she said, patting her huge thighs and holding one of her enormous breasts with both of her veiny, silver-nailed hands. "Isn't that right, you crazy old man?" she laughed in a loud and vulgar way.

"Of course," said Domínguez, caressing her curly, yellowish hair. "But bring him a fresh young one who doesn't have all those nasty habits you do."

"No trouble," she said, patting Rogelio's cheek lightly.

She gestured with her head for them to follow her. She led them to a room where soft red light revealed a large, comfortable dark sofa and a coffee table.

"This is the Red Room, your favorite, old man. Have a seat. I'll send some girls to take care of you. Have fun."

"This is the life," said Domínguez, lighting a cigarette. "A real oasis. Did you know this is one of the best brothels in the capital?"

"Is the fat woman the owner?"

"She's just the administrator. Not even she knows who the owner is," he whispered to Rogelio. "They bring her young girls from small towns and villages, for her to get them started in the business."

"Who brings them?"

"People who control the underworld. They kidnap girls from the country. They run several houses of prostitution in the city, of a variety of categories and prices. A great business, don't you think?"

"Great corruption. Excellent material for writing a good article and denouncing it publicly."

"That'd be a waste of time. The business of prostitution is public and common knowledge. Of course it's an immoral profession, but you've got to admit it makes economic sense."

"Poor women," said the young man, sitting down. "They're slaves. They're exploited."

"Oh, stop it, man. Don't act so bitter. These women are smarter than you and I together. Don't be such a prude. At least they aren't out on the street begging. They have a place to stay and something to eat. They live better than many Salvadorans who don't have even a straw mat to fall dead on. Did you know that prostitution is the world's oldest profession?"

"Where's that music coming from?"

"From the ceiling," said Domínguez, sitting down on the sofa. "The music covers up the conversations. That's why you can talk and shout freely here. This is open territory for, among other things, talking all kinds of nonsense without being incriminated.

"Hi," said a young woman in a transparent dress who came in carrying a tray full of bottles of beer and glasses. "Nice to see you, Domínguez," she said, placing everything on the table.

After the young woman left, Rogelio poured the beer and gave a glass to Domínguez. "Looks like you're quite well-known around here," he commented.

"This is where I come to leave my paycheck and my troubles. I leave here drunk and free of conflicts. If not for this place, I'd be locked up in a nuthouse by now, or maybe I'd have killed someone, if not myself."

"And I thought you were a practical man with no serious problems!"

"I have more problems than the government junta," he said, emptying his glass in a single gulp. "But I'm not an animal either. I have my sensitivity, my guilt complex. But with time, and fear, I've learned to hide my emotions and play the fool. But I must tell you that since you've been working with me, I've been feeling somewhat depressed."

"Why? I thought you were pleased with my work."

"I'm not complaining about your work; on the contrary, it impresses me. What I mean is that I envy the sincerity and enthusiasm with which you confront life, your faith in human beings, your hope for the future."

"When I was a child, I learned that if we don't have faith we live blindly. We limit our time and space. We must believe in something or someone, above all in ourselves, because we accomplish nothing by being fatalistic."

"You remind me of my own youth, when I wrote my first articles and suffered my first rude awakening. I had glorious dreams. I dreamed of being a great reporter. I thought I had the world by the tail. Do you know who one of my heroes was?"

"Who?"

"None other than Ortega y Gasset. I read and reread all his works. I swore to myself that I would become better than he. And I had a deep conviction that I could do it. But, look what I've become... A liar... An insensitive drunk..."

"It's not your fault, Domínguez. It's been proven a thousand times that here no one can aspire to excel in anything, especially if you're poor. Sooner or later everyone's wings are clipped."

"But then it's better to stop as soon as you realize that you can't fulfill your dreams, and not wait to end up old and bitter."

"But then why are you pushing me to be a reporter? So I'll fall into the same trap? Don't forget, I only work at *The Tribune* out of economic necessity, not because I'm interested in journalism."

"It's just that when I see your energy, I think that maybe times have changed, or will change soon, that maybe you'll have better luck than I did. Understand? Your hopes and dreams are now mine. I admire your good will, your sense of justice...your faith; and I feel a certain joy now when I think that I was once like you. Rogelio, you are a mirror of my own youth. On the other hand, I'm all washed up. I'm a useless old man, who can't even look back for fear that the memories will turn him into a salt statue, like Lot's wife."

"What a bitter comparison."

"It's just that things are getting so violent," sighed Domínguez, suddenly seeming to sink into sadness. "We're entering a tunnel with no way out. And it hurts me, more than anything, for our young people who are being left with no alternative other than chaos, violence and death. What kind of future is that? It infuriates me to see young ideals being destroyed. For example, do you think that your disillusionment, your realization that journalism in this country is an empty, irrelevant exercise having nothing to do with reality, didn't hurt me deeply? Of course it did!"

CABINET MEMBERS DENOUNCE MILITARY INTER-
FERENCE IN NEW GOVERNMENT. MONSIGNOR
ROMERO INTERVENES SO THAT ARMED FORCES
HIGH COMMAND AND GOVERNMENT JUNTA MAY
DISCUSS THEIR DIFFERENCES IN THE EPISCOPAL
OFFICE.

As was the custom on Sundays, the vast majority of radios in the country were tuned to YSAX, the station that broadcast Sunday Mass from the Metropolitan Cathedral. It was a tradition. Everyone stopped their daily chores, in the city and in the country, in the poor slums, the middle-class neighborhoods and the sumptuous mansions, to listen to the homily of Monsignor Romero, Archbishop of San Salvador, whose message was heard even beyond the nation's borders.

Monsignor Romero: Moved by the word of God and by the great deal of violence that has affected different sectors of our country, I am obliged to issue a new call to all Christians and persons of good will, that we may reflect upon the present situation in our country and act responsibly to save it from falling into outright civil war.

I am going to present the facts to you and then, with pastoral judgment, we will try to analyze them.

It is evident that at this time in El Salvador, three economic-political projects exist which are in conflict with one another. And each wants to be the only one to prevail.

First, *the oligarchical project* which is attempting to employ all of its immense economic power to prevent the implementation of structural reforms which affect its interests but which favor the majority of Salvadorans. This system seeks, through economic and political pressure, and even through violence, to maintain the current economic-oligarchic structure, which is obviously unjust and has become unbearable. To date it has managed to attract a sector of private enterprise and also, evidently, a sector of the Army, to help defend its oligarchical interests. It is rumored that in addition they have hired mercenaries to fight unscrupulously against any other force which attempts to redistribute national wealth and income. And it has again ordered the bloody and criminal acts of the paramilitary group UGB. It is already in action.

Second, *the governmental project promoted by the Armed Forces and the Christian Democratic Party*. In spite of having published a manifesto which further specified the proclamation of the Armed Forces with an anti-oligarchical popular posture, and in spite of having promised to carry out structural reforms, to date, in practice, it has been incapable of unifying the sectors, the popular organizations, and instead has dedicated itself to indiscriminately and disproportionately repressing and massacring peasants and other groups of people as is happening, for example, in the area of Arcatao.

Third, *the third project presented is that of the popular and political-military organizations*. This project is rapidly tending toward unity and has issued a call to all democratic organizations, progressive persons, small- and medium-business people, conscientious members of the military, to form a wide and powerful group of revolutionary and democratic forces to make it possible for democracy and social justice to reign in our country. A popular project, which has already initiated a process of unity and coordination among the different popular and political-military organizations, but which still needs to make this invitation to the democratic and progressive sectors more explicit, it is a wide union that truly seeks the common good of the country and tries to the utmost to avoid violence, vengeance, and all those activities that extend or intensify the bloodshed.

Regarding these three political-economic projects, the pastoral judgment which I believe I must make is this.

Above all, we must first remember once more that the Church's duty is not to identify with one project or another, nor to be a leader of an eminently political process. I wrote in the Fourth Pastoral Letter, and today this thought seems very appropriate: "What is truly important to the Church is to offer the country the light of the Gospel for the complete salvation and uplifting of man. A salvation which also includes the structures in which man lives, so they do not hinder him, but rather help him, to live the life of a son of God." This is the mission of the Church, one that is totally evangelical. No community or pastoral agent can say which project is best for a particular Christian community. The Church must only evangelically advocate for man and in this way strive to uplift him, even on this earth, working, inspiring, so that the structures themselves may favor this complete uplifting of man. Therefore, then, the light with which we illuminate these projects that I have mentioned is a light of an evangelical and moral nature.

Concretely, with respect to the first project, the oligarchical one: I cannot approve, but rather must disapprove... Disapprove of the conduct of those people who, in defending their privileges and accumulated wealth and in not wanting to share them in a brotherly manner with all Salvadorans, are making the possibility of resolving the structural crisis in a peaceful way even more remote. I allow myself to remind this oligarchical sector once more of the teaching of Medellín. Medellín says: "If you jealously defend your privileges and, above all, if you defend them by employing violent means, you become responsible to history for provoking the explosive revolutions of desperation..." The peaceful future of El Salvador depends, in large part, on your attitudes.

The economically powerful should also remember these words of John Paul II in his inaugural speech in Puebla. The Pope said: "The Church does indeed defend the legitimate right to private property, but it teaches, with no less clarity, that there is always a social mortgage recorded on all private property..." The image is precious: "No one can have any property without its being mortgaged; it is mortgaged to the common good..." And that, says the Pope, is so that all property may serve the purpose God has given it. "And if the common good demands it—words of the Pope—one must not hesitate at the thought of expropriation done in the proper manner..."

Editor's office. The door opens suddenly; six men enter.

Leader (shouts): Who's the boss here?

Domínguez: I am, at your service.

(Immediately two men grab him and, in a matter of seconds, handcuff him.)

Domínguez: What's going on? What is this?

Leader: You're going with us. We just want to ask you some questions.

Domínguez: Questions? What kind of questions? Who are you?

(The one closest to the editor gives him a sharp kick in the stomach.)

Man No. 1 (scornfully): Don't ask so many questions, you old bastard!

Man No. 2 (threatening, aiming his revolver at Rogelio): And you, don't move, unless you want to die right there!

(The editor has fallen to the floor and is moaning. His wrinkled face is bleeding badly. The photographer enters the office, attracted by the shouts and, seeing Domínguez on the floor, attempts to help him, but a kick in the back stops him, sending him rolling under a table. His equipment crashes to the floor, shattering into pieces. He tries to get up, but a blow to the head leaves him lying next to the editor.)

Man No. 3: If you get in the way again, you die, son-of-a-bitch! This is none of your business!

(The leader observes the scene calmly, stationed at the door.)

Leader (shouts): Grab the old man and let's go!

They rush out of the office, dragging Domínguez. Seconds later, alarmed, other employees enter the office. The director arrives also and goes toward the photographer, who is lying unconscious on the floor.)

Director: What the hell is going on here!

(Rogelio finally leaves the corner behind his desk and goes toward the director.)

Rogelio (terrified): Some men came and took Domínguez away! They said they wanted to ask him some questions, but when he asked for an explanation they beat him. Ramos tried to help him and they hit him, too.

(Two of the employees pick up the photographer and carry him out of the office.)

Director: This is a crime! We must report it immediately through all the media!

Administrator: We must notify any influential people we know. But it has to be immediately, before it's too late.

Director: Each of us must contact as many people as we can. The important thing is to make Domínguez' arrest public in order to protect his life!

(The employees leave the office, mentioning names of important persons who might be able to help. Rogelio paces in the office, completely disoriented, yet understanding that he has to do something, anything, and soon. His eyes search the office desperately, and come to rest on a photograph of Monsignor Romero that hangs on the wall. Rogelio goes closer to read the Archbishop's handwritten dedication to Domínguez, whom Rogelio once heard speak of his friendship with the priest. He goes to his desk, picks up the telephone, and dials.)

Rogelio: Is this the Archbishop's office? I must speak with Monsignor Romero! It's a matter of life and death!

Secretary's voice (calm and quiet): Hello, who's calling? Monsignor isn't here right now. How can we help you?

Rogelio (desperately): I have to talk to him! A journalist at *The Tribune*, whom Monsignor knows, has just been arrested.

Secretary's Voice: Who?

Rogelio: Domínguez!

Secretary's voice: The editor?

Rogelio: Yes.

Secretary's voice: Monsignor is out of town for a few days...

Rogelio: But what should I do? I can't waste time. His life is in danger!

Secretary's voice: The best thing is for you to go to the place where you believe he is being held. In the meantime, we will mobilize some contacts...

Rogelio: We don't even know why they've arrested him! They said they just wanted to ask him some questions.

Secretary's voice: I'm sorry to tell you this, but that is quite common now. Nevertheless, we mustn't lose hope. With God's help we'll get him released...

Rogelio: God willing!

(He rushes out of the office, slamming the door behind him.)

We arrived in Ilobasco as the sun was beginning to set behind the hills. The bus bounced around on the narrow stone streets of the placid hamlet I knew so well, my home. When I was a child I would play right in the middle of the road, since cars almost never went by, only carts. I would pick up a stone to reveal a hole and tiny crabs of different colors would come out. I remember once I found a gold one. I took it in my hands and it disappeared. I started to cry because I had wanted to take it home, to make my brother jealous. Ah! The memories of childhood!

I asked the driver to stop and let us out in front of a house with red doors and white-washed walls. The door opened and my mother, followed by my father, came out to meet us. My mother and I hugged each other. I held out my hands to my father, who kissed me on the forehead as we embraced.

He shook Rogelio's hand warmly.

"What a pleasure to meet you! Come in please, make yourself at home. My name is Arístides."

"Come right in," my mother said to Rogelio. "My name is Pilar. It's so nice to meet you. Lourdes has told us a lot about you. Have a seat."

"Thank you; you're very kind," said Rogelio.

"Would you like something to drink?" my father asked. "Pilar, bring us some juice, please. How was your trip? No problems?"

Rogelio began by telling him the incident of the Guardsman interested in the portrait. My mother returned with drinks and put them on the coffee table.

"Help yourself, please, Rogelio," she said. "Would you like a sweet roll?"

"Thank you."

As we enjoyed the tamarind drink, Rogelio was studying the walls, which were full of decorations of many shapes and colors. My father, noticing his interest in a clay urn adorned with three-dimensional red serpents, took some other pieces out of a trunk to show him.

"We make these, too," he said proudly. "They are considered to be the most original works in all of Ilobasco."

"They are truly lovely," affirmed Rogelio, taking them in his hands. "In design as well as in color."

"I myself carved the molds for these statues, a long time ago. Come, I'll show you some more."

They excused themselves and left. I saw them enter the kitchen, which leads to the central patio, which is large and contains a great variety of flowers and plants. In the center there is a fountain from which crystalline water flows into a pool.

"Your father described to me the shops where they make the clay figures," Rogelio commented to me later. "I was dazzled by the garden. The patio looked like a piece of paradise and I told your father so. The cool breeze carried the perfume of the flowers. The trees were full of birds and their warbling. Beautiful!

"'This is my favorite place in the whole house,' said your father, and, at that moment, I suddenly stopped and almost screamed: And what is *that*?

"'Those are the statues that my son, Remigio, makes.'

"I approached the sculptures and became tense, paralyzed, my skin crawling and my ears ringing.

"'God, they look real,' I stammered, thinking: How horrible! 'Your son is a sculptor? Lourdes never told me about him.'

"'She must have wanted to surprise you,' he said, stroking the huge belly of the statue of the Cipitío. 'Remigio has made many, but I think these are the best.'

"I went closer. There was the Siguanaba of the stories which had caused me so much fear when I was a child and which still, in spite of my 30 years, seemed to frighten me. A swollen face with enormous round eyes, long eyelashes and thick eyebrows. A large mouth with horse-like teeth and fleshy lips. Long shining hair that reached almost to her knees. Full breasts which rested on a bulging stomach with a large navel. Hairy, muscular arms and disproportionately long hands, with bony fingers and sharp black fingernails. There was that woman who, according to the legends, would wait for men on the riverbank to seduce them, make love to them, and then put her spell on them, leaving them bewitched. There was the horrible woman, next to her naked, big-bellied son, dwarflike and with huge teeth, wearing a gigantic hat on his head, as if he were an immense mushroom.

"'I want to show you the idols I told you about,' said your father, giving me a pat on the shoulder which broke the spell that seemed to have come over me.

"'Yes, yes, let's go,' I managed to say, almost tripping over a stone, rubbing my eyes, and lighting a cigarette to try to hide my confusion."

THREE CIVILIAN MEMBERS OF THE JUNTA AND 34 MEMBERS OF THE CABINET RESIGN "IN PROTEST AGAINST EXCESSIVE MILITARY INFLUENCE IN THE GOVERNMENT."

Monsignor Romero: With respect to the second project, the government project. First, I quote some judgments of former government officials, so that you and the people may judge objectively. According to these former government officials, the possibilities of introducing reformist solutions in alliance with the current leadership of the Armed Forces, controlled by pro-oligarchic elements and not having any real popular participation, have been exhausted. The solution which they, the former officials, propose, is establishing a democratic regime that is truly committed to social justice... which requires as a fundamental element—these are their words—"as a fundamental element requires the participation and direction of the people, their popular and democratic organizations, and truly confronting the oligarchy and their allies..."

I believe that the members of the Christian Democratic Party and the other participants in the current government should pay great attention to the opinion of these experienced ex-officials who, together with the members of the military who have not yet abandoned their dreams of change and justice, must enter into a dialogue with the popular organizations and other democratic progressive organizations or sectors so that they may work on finding a way to create this broad Government proposed by the popular organizations themselves and by some ex-functionaries, based not on the present Armed Forces but rather on the organized consensus of the majority of the people…because a Government that promises change and social justice, yet stains itself more and more each day with the alarming reports, that come to us from all areas, of harsh repression and the killing of people, as is the case in Las Vueltas and Arcatao, can never prevail.

You can read the facts today in Orientation. I won't take up your time, but what has happened in those regions of Arcatao is something very cruel. Under the pretext of avenging or looking for a disappeared Guardsman and of detecting pockets of guerrillas, the rural population is being threatened and killed indiscriminately. I recognize that the assassination of persons only because they are members of the organization ORDEN or the National Guard is a senseless and condemnable act. I already denounced this crime last Sunday when I issued a call to avoid lighting the spark there. And I condemn it again today, but the disproportionate nature of the punishment that is being inflicted on the peasants, many of whom are innocent, is truly appalling.

I received a letter from the wife of this Guardsman. And I believe that as human beings we must feel this pain. She found out about her husband's tragedy precisely through our homily, last Sunday. She hadn't known anything about it before. And afterward she wrote to me, and delivered the letter herself: "With my gaze set on God and on you, I come with these humble words to beg once more, although you have already done so once, that you intercede on behalf of my husband, José Elías Torres Quintanilla, National Guardsman, who was kidnapped January 12 of this year by elements of a clandestine organization as he traveled from Arcatao to Chalatenango, and to date I do not know his whereabouts. I hope that your assistance may alleviate my anguish as a wife and as the mother of an eight-month-old son; we need my husband. God will repay you for all your goodness and for what you do on our behalf." Last night I heard rumors, I don't know if they have been confirmed, that the body of this disappeared Guardsman had been found. This we will never approve of; it is a crime. And the Pope says: "We must call things by their proper names."

There is an eyewitness commentary of what is happening there. It says: "We—a peasant writes to me—are very sad because presently in this department there has been unleashed one of the cruelest persecutions and massacres against the peasants, men, women, children, etc., who have been mistreated by the authorities and members of ORDEN, creating a panic never before seen in this Northern region. We have verified this personally, because here where we live we are surrounded by refugees, who have come with only the clothes on their backs, having neither a place to live nor permission to return to their homes, where they have abandoned everything. Their houses have been plundered, some burned, their animals stolen or killed with machetes, their crops destroyed, and an endless number of other things have been done to these people, whose only crime is that of being poor and organized."

Also, one of the nuns, when she left, wrote me: "We leave sadly because we see that this is not only an act of retaliation for the capture of a member of the National Guard, but that the situation is being taken advantage of to conduct repression of the people planned previously at a high level of authority. The price the people are having to pay, in blood, for their liberation hurts us deeply, a price that as Christians we cannot accept but, when there is no other solution, one in which we find meaning when we place it next to the crucified Lord so that it can attain its redemptive value..."

The Government Junta should order, in an effective manner, an immediate stop to so much indiscriminate repression, because the Junta is also responsible for the blood, the pain of so many people. The Armed Forces, especially the security forces, should lay aside the brutality and hatred with which they persecute the people; they should demonstrate by their actions that they are in favor of the majority and that the process they have initiated is popular in nature. Many of you military personnel are of humble origin, and therefore the Army as an institution should be at the service of the people. Do not destroy the people, do not provoke the greater and more painful outbreaks of violence with which a repressed people could justly respond...

I have a very expressive letter from a group of soldiers. Very revealing! I will read the part which may interest us most: "We, a group of soldiers, ask you to make public our problems and the demands we present to the officers and chiefs and the Government Junta, and in anticipation of your help we will be grateful. What we want is to try to attain the betterment of the troops of the Armed Forces of El Salvador:

1st) improvement of the food;

2nd) that beating and humiliation of the troops be avoided;

3rd) that the uniforms of the troops be improved;

4th) that our salary be increased, because what we actually receive is 20 or 30 colones per month, and after all the deductions they take from us we are left with nothing;

5th) that we not be sent to repress the population... Dear soldiers, this applause of the people represents a hand reaching out to you in your anguish;

6th) they continue asking—that clothing maintenance not be deducted from us;

7th) that we be told why we are being sent into combat...

8th) the Armed Forces are made up of troops, chiefs, and officers, and it is only the chiefs and officers who are responsible for all the oppression done to the people;...

9th) that our life insurance be increased, which currently is 2,000 colones;

10th) and lastly, to issue a call to the people in general: workers, peasants, students, and all the
   unions and popular revolutionary organizations, asking that you support us in our struggle to achieve our betterment, and in
   exchange, we take responsibility for assuring
   that the Armed Forces protect and defend the
   interests of the people, and not of the rich as
   has been the case until now..."

A woman entered the Red Room carrying a tray full of beer bottles and glasses. Domínguez took her by the arm and sat her down on his lap.

"You're already drunk, crazy old man," she said, laughing. "Stop pawing me. You know you're too old for these things."

She managed to get away and left with the empty bottles. The fat woman came to inquire:

"Is everything all right? Are they taking good care of you?"

"Of course, Gordita," said Domínguez. "Everything's perfect. Will you have a little drink with us?"

"I can't right now, but 'another time it will be,' like the song says. I have to keep an eye on things and make sure the customers are taken care of."

"Don't be that way, Gordita," he insisted, pulling her toward him and caressing her. "Have a little drink, don't be difficult."

"Let me go, you crazy old man. I can't right now; don't be so stubborn. I'll be sending you a couple of women right away."

The fat woman left and, minutes later, two young women appeared. One of them sat down next to Domínguez.

"Oh! Don't tell me you're reporters!"

"Yes, we're reporters. Poor reporters," said Domínguez.

"Ah, I understand," she said, perhaps not understanding Domínguez' sarcasm. "All kinds come here. Rich men, soldiers, and rebels. But all of them end up drunk and going to bed with one of us."

"At least here they all agree on something," interrupted Rogelio who, not used to drinking, was beginning to feel the effect of the beer. It seemed to him that everything was spinning around him.

"Come here, girl," Domínguez said to the other woman who was still standing in the middle of the room, timidly, as if unfamiliar with that environment. "Sit down; don't be shy."

She still remained at a distance from the group, and Domínguez insisted: "Come here, precious. Don't be afraid of us; we aren't going to do anything bad to you."

"Come on; sit down," urged Rogelio, moving over to make room for her on the sofa.

Finally the girl sat down next to Rogelio.

"What are the little girls going to drink?" asked Domínguez.

"Little girls? You've got to be kidding!" the one who said her name was Chata said jokingly, sitting down next to Domínguez.

"A little whiskey? Yes?" offered the boss. "Take advantage today while I'm a big spender; tomorrow I won't have even enough for beans."

"I don't want anything," answered the one who was next to Rogelio.

"Well, I do want a good drink," said Chata. "And don't worry about her; she's very unsociable. She doesn't talk, doesn't drink, doesn't smoke. Her name is Soledad. She only likes...look at what I mean," she said, making gestures which, in a vulgar way, described sexual acts.

"This Chata sure is funny," laughed Domínguez.

"I'll go get some more drinks," said Soledad, still in a bad mood, as she got up and left the room.

"Don't let her bother you," Chata told Rogelio as she sat down on Domínguez' lap. "Just take her to bed. They say she's really good."

"She's pretty," agreed the boss.

"She's very young," added Chata. "They brought her here three weeks ago and it's going really well for her. All the men come back for her."

"Go for it, man!" Domínguez said to Rogelio. "Don't waste time! I'm going with you, my dear little Chata."

"Whenever you like. I love crazy old men like you."

"Here are the drinks," said Soledad, returning and putting the glasses on the table.

"Excellent!" said Chata after downing the drink in one swallow. "I'll have another one!"

"Wait a minute; drink it slowly," said Domínguez, getting up. "Or else you'll get drunk too soon."

"Nothing gets me drunk."

"Later I'll buy you another, my darling Chata. But now we'd better go to your room."

"Let's go then, old man," she gave in, laughing, and they left the room with their arms around each other.

Dinner was served and we sat down at the table. My brother came in and I got up to hug him. Rogelio shook his hand, said "Nice to meet you," and when he did not get a response thought his presence made my brother uncomfortable, but after a few minutes he realized that Remigio was a deaf-mute.

During dinner, my brother smiled as if he understood our words. We cleared the table and served coffee. We chatted for more than an hour about various subjects, including the current situation in our country. Remigio's yawns indicated that it was time to go to bed. My mother showed Rogelio to his room, we said good night, and each of us went to our own room.

"Lying there in the dark," Rogelio told me afterward, "I thought about the solutions to our country's problems that your father explained during dinner. His concepts were clear, but seemed like illusions that could never be realized in our circumstances. Perhaps for that reason he expressed them with a certain sorrow, like someone who knows the medicine that could cure the fatal illness of someone who prefers to die rather than try the medicine. My country is so strange! A land where talents are wasted and despised!

"Finally my thoughts yielded to my weariness, and I fell asleep to the sounds of the crickets and the frogs.

"Several hours later, I was awakened by the sound of whispering and soft laughter, which seemed to be coming from the garden. I listened. The noise was coming and going. My curiosity made me get up and, walking slowly, I went to stand behind one of the pillars in the courtyard. The weak light of the moon spread over the garden, illuminating it enough to allow me to make out the pool and its beautiful fountain in the center of the patio.

"The laughter began again. I tried to see where it was coming from and my gaze fell on the fountain, where it seemed to me that the statues of the Siguanaba and the Cipitío were moving. I couldn't believe it, and I rubbed my eyes trying to see more clearly. My surprise was even greater when I saw your brother embracing the Siguanaba. The woman was laughing in an evil way, kissing him with those thick lips that I couldn't see but imagined. Slowly she slid across the grass near the fountain, grabbed Remigio around the waist and pulled him toward her. The Cipitío climbed up on the fountain and, while he urinated, he moved his head which was covered with an enormous hat. His eyes shone like luminous points which threw off great rays of light onto the garden; perhaps he was keeping watch so the lovers would not be discovered.

"I felt intense chills. My fear of making noise and interrupting that macabre love scene, provoking the anger of those strange characters, made me return to my bed. My body trembled as I listened to the whispers and mischievous laughter which did not stop until the first rooster crowed.

"I couldn't fall asleep. I wasn't brave enough to dare to leave my room again. Even when the sun's first rays appeared and I heard that people were beginning to get up, I didn't stick my head out into the hall.

"I remember, Lourdes, that you came to see me. The morning sun had already flooded the room; nevertheless, when I heard you come in, I pretended to be asleep."

"You opened your eyes when I kissed your forehead. I remember that I said 'Good morning, did you sleep well?'"

"'Yes, I slept great, and you?' I responded, thinking that, while you answered, I would have time to decide if I should tell you about my discovery or not."

"As soon as I lay down and closed my eyes, I fell right asleep. No problem."

"'Me, too,' I lied, since at that moment I concluded that I couldn't tell you anything about your brother's secret love because you would laugh and tell me it was just a dream. Besides, Lourdes, I knew that the possibility existed that it had all been just another of my usual nightmares."

"I remember that my mother knocked on your door to give you a towel, and pointed out that the bathroom was across the patio."

"That's right, and I left the room."

"Then she said that the water in the fountain was cool and that perhaps you would prefer to wash your face there."

"And I immediately responded that I would go to the bathroom. I crossed the patio keeping my gaze far from the statues. But when I passed in front of them I felt my skin crawl. In the bathroom I met your brother and said good morning to him. He responded with a wide smile that revealed his crooked, yellow teeth. With his index finger he pointed to the statues and then to himself. I nodded with an uncertain smile since, Lourdes, I wasn't sure if Remigio was telling me that he had made them, or that he was in love with that horrible woman."

"What town are you from?" asked Rogelio as he served himself another beer in spite of being very drunk already.

"Amatillo," murmured Soledad who, until then, had been sitting in silence on the other end of the sofa, her gaze fixed on the floor.

"What?" he asked, his head spinning.

"Amatillo."

"Amatillo in La Union? Amatillo on the border?"

"Yes, the Honduran border. Why?"

"Because that's where I'm from," he responded through uncontrollable hiccoughs which did not lend the least bit of credibility to his words.

"Don't joke, please. There's no reason to be telling me stories. If you want to go to bed with me, just pay and that's it."

"But it's true. My name is Rogelio Villaverde," he insisted, moving closer to her.

Although she was backing away from him, Soledad asked, "And your father, what's his name?"

"His name was Angel, my mother Inocencia and my brothers Rómulo and Evaristo."

Recovering her expression, which only seconds earlier seemed so icy, she answered dryly, "I don't believe you."

"I have no reason to lie to you."

The color began to return to her pale face; for the first time she showed some emotion.

"It's just that, if it's true..." she stuttered.

"Why are you so surprised at what I'm telling you?"

"Because, if what you say is true, I knew your family."

"What?"

Now Rogelio was the surprised one. He suddenly regretted being drunk at such a critical moment.

"I knew them..." Soledad's face grew somber again.

"What? You knew my family? How? When? Explain."

He was struggling to understand what she was telling him and to recover from his intoxicated state.

"Yes, I met them in Honduras."

"You what?" It was again his turn to be incredulous, and the impact of those revelations seemed to diminish his drunkenness.

"Yes, believe me; I knew them. They had crossed the border and were living in Honduras, on a small plot of land next to my family. We were neighbors. When the problems started we decided to flee, but we were ambushed on the way. Some of us ran and managed to escape through the brush. I remember that all I could hear were shots. Almost dead from exhaustion and fear, I fainted at the edge of a path. Other Salvadorans who were fleeing picked me up. I crossed the border with them and finally we arrived in El Salvador."

Hiding her face under the sofa pillows, she began to sob like an abandoned child.

"It's all over now. Don't worry," Rogelio tried to console her. "You're safe now; that's what matters."

His words of consolation competed with the music and the shouts of two clients who, having had too many drinks, were fighting over a woman who did not want to go to bed with either of them.

Soledad continued moaning and sighing. The surprising story had alleviated Rogelio's headache and drunkenness considerably.

"Do you smoke?" He offered her a cigarette. She did not answer.

"My family went to Honduras because where we lived there were no jobs," said Rogelio. "Several relatives who were already established there used to tell us about the abundance of abandoned land that anyone could cultivate. I went to San Salvador. Later I went to try my luck in the United States. When I heard about the war, I returned immediately in search of my family. I went to several villages and refugee camps, but I didn't find anyone. Completely disillusioned, without the slightest idea of my family's fate, I returned to the United States."

Tears began to roll down Rogelio's cheeks also.

"I couldn't find my family either," said Soledad. "Since I was orphaned, they let me live in a refugee camp. One day I became sick and they took me to the hospital. When I got better, I no longer had anywhere to live. The hospital doorman got me a room in a boarding house, which he paid for while he took advantage of me. Months later I became pregnant and he left me. When my son was born, I couldn't support him and I had to abandon him. I remember that when I left him at the gate of the church, I said this prayer: My God who gave me this son, I cannot take care of him, and since he is also your son..."

She couldn't continue. Her lips were trembling and for a moment her words were reduced to sobs.

"A few days later the police found me sleeping in a doorway and took me to jail. The chief of the jail, a lieutenant who would take me to his room almost every night, got them to accept me in an orphanage, where I stayed for about five years. Once when they took us to a town fair, some men kidnapped four of us girls from the orphanage, brought us to the capital, and forced us to work in these places in San Salvador."

"How long have they had you here?"

"About four years. They send us to different places every three months."

"How old are you?"

"I'm not sure, but I think I'm 24."

Their conversation was abruptly interrupted by the Gorda.

"Okay, Saintly Face, what'll it be?" she asked, approaching Rogelio and caressing his hair. "Don't talk so much; you aren't boyfriend and girlfriend and this isn't a park. If you aren't going to bed with Soledad, I have to take her to another room. There's an Army man there asking for her. Soledad, you remember that Colonel who gives you presents and takes you to Tamarindo Beach." Soledad tried to ignore Gorda's words and looked at the floor. "Well, that same one keeps asking and asking for you. Tell me the secret, girl. What do you give to these men who are always going around looking for you like dogs in heat?"

"We're going right now; she's just having a drink," said Rogelio, putting a glass of beer in Soledad's cold hands. She looked at him pleadingly, as if begging him not to abandon her.

"Don't waste time," Gorda scolded. "Soledad hasn't gone to bed with anyone tonight. And she knows very well that she's here to work and make money."

"We're going right now," said Rogelio, taking Soledad's arm.

"That's better, Saintly Face! Like a real macho man!" exclaimed Gorda, and then she told Soledad: "Give him good service, like I've taught you. And behave yourself, because if you don't, you know what'll happen to you, little girl."

Rogelio followed Soledad's steps down dark, narrow hallways flanked by rooms from which laughter of women and shouts of drunken men could be heard. An impassioned Javier Solís song was playing: "What good is my soul, if it is already bitter..." Soledad stopped and unlocked a door.

"Come in, sir," she said, turning on the light. "Come in, please; this is my house." Her face became sad again, and from her moist, red eyes big tears fell to the floor forming asterisks. "There's the bed; sit down." She closed the door and sighed. "Do you like my house? I'll be right with you, just a moment, please," she said, doing all she could to sing along with the words of the song that could be heard from the room next door. "Singing drives away evil, right, sir? Sit down, don't worry, I'll be right with you."

She fell silent for an instant and then, with the same sad voice, accompanied the song: "Why be good if they laugh in your face, may the current carry me away, may the current carry me away, I will never return..."

Domínguez: They pushed me out of the office and threw me into a station wagon and drove away fast. Face down, on the filthy floor of that mobile prison, my soul was terrified; I felt a sensation not of pain but rather of breathing the hot air of a tomb. I tried to remember the best moments of my life and in that way console myself in my anguish. More than anything I tried to convince myself that my existence, soon to end, had had some purpose. I searched the whirlpool of my memory hoping to find something that would justify the effort of having lived. Because without having lived fully for at least one moment, life has no meaning and therefore dying has no meaning either.

We arrived at Headquarters and they took me out of the vehicle. I walked along, silently pronouncing a resigned farewell to life. I was sure that not even my remains would ever leave this place for the cemetery, but I thanked God for having given me more than fifty years of existence. I thought that, given the critical situation of things, that was enough.

We went through the main door. Two men marched in front of me and another followed me, the three of them in complete silence, like bearers of a message only too well known for them, the repetition of which took the shine off it, converting it into mere routine.

We walked though gloomy hallways, and from the closed rooms I could hear the sounds of beatings, mixed with raucous laughter and screams begging for pity.

Armed men escorting prisoners came and went through the hallways. We, the unfortunate ones, when we passed one another, exchanged expressions of resignation and mutual pity. The Biblical scene of Jesus carrying his heavy cross to Calvary came to my mind. Although the prisoners here carried no wooden crosses, nor were there women and children throwing flowers in our path, our destiny was the same. Finally we stopped and they knocked on a door. "Come in!" someone shouted from inside, and the cutting tone of the voice immediately put my nerves on edge. We went in, they saluted and gave their report and then, shoving me, without taking off the handcuffs, they made me sit on a small bench.

The bindings had made my hands numb to the point that I couldn't even feel them anymore, but from the moment they handcuffed me, I had resigned myself to that. They are only my arms and hands, I was thinking. I already know what they are like and what their function is; so, in this state, they are no good to me. I began to have the same thoughts about my feet, because they were useless to me as well. My whole body was an obstacle, because these men would mistreat it, unaware that my resignation to die had made it immune to suffering. In this situation, resignation is like a powerful shield that protects the soul from the most dreadful bodily harm. You feel yourself become only spirit, space; you become detached from your body and its filth. This whirlwind of confused ideas plagued my mind and tortured me psychologically, although up to that moment I had not suffered too much physically.

I noticed that an officer, seated behind a desk, was examining some papers. With expressions and movements that were obviously practiced, he lit a cigarette and blew lightly to put out the match.

"I'm going to ask you some questions," he said with the cigarette in his mouth, "and you're going to give true answers, that is, answers that convince me; and if you don't, you already know what awaits you... As editor-in-chief of *The Tribune*, you must remember that last week you published an article about the possibility of a military uprising against the Government Junta. I want you to tell me the plain, clear truth about who gave you that information."

I answered without hesitation that the article came from several international press reports. The reports arrive at the newspaper from the whole world, the editors compile them, I correct them, the director approves them, and they are published. That is the normal process that...

"But *The Tribune* was the only paper that carried that news!" he interrupted, suddenly getting up.

"But that news had already been divulged on the radio and on television much earlier," I said. "It was old news."

"The article declares that the United States will not permit the countercoup. How do you know that? Perhaps you work for the gringos?"

"No," I said. "That article was based on the fact, well-known to the whole world, that the United States has promised to support the Government Junta in order to maintain a moderate center and at the same time soften up the right and counteract the ultra-left, all of which is public knowledge and no secret."

The interrogator slammed his fist on the desk. "I see that you don't want to cooperate. Don't make me resort to extreme measures. Think—at your age you couldn't stand a beating. Therefore, let's go on, we'll see how you respond to the second question." He took a recent edition of *The Tribune* out of his desk and with his index finger pointed to the headline 'Arms Traffic.' "According to this report," he said, "there exists in this country a black market in which weapons belonging to the National Army are bought and sold, and this black market supplies the guerrillas. How do you know that?"

"Through an international press report," I answered, "and we published it after the news was heard on a local radio station. This is news as normal as any other kind..."

The interrogator approached me slowly, pointing at me with his lighted cigarette. "That kind of news subverts public order, as you know very well; that's why you published it."

"No," I answered, "it's common, ordinary news, that has no purpose other than to inform the public that there is illegal arms traffic, from which a few benefit and which feeds the general violence that harms us all..."

"Tell me the truth!" screamed the interrogator. "Don't make me lose my patience because you'll be sorry. You're involved in the arms traffic to supply the guerrillas!"

"No," I responded, "I only publish the news..."

"Now you're going to tell me who your contacts are!"

"I know nothing about any arms business, believe me, sir!"

Without even listening to me, he signalled to the man who was closest to me, who, with a surprise movement, dealt me such a powerful blow in the side that he made me fall and roll on the floor with a scream of pain.

"You bring the arms from Cuba to Nicaragua, don't you?"

"No, I don't know anything about that," I answered, trying vainly to get up.

"And then you send them to Guatemala and from there to El Salvador where they distribute them to the guerrillas? Isn't that right?!"

"I don't know anything about that!" I shouted. "I'm not an arms smuggler, believe me! I'm innocent of those charges! I'm just a journalist!"

"Tell me the names of your bosses and contacts. If you cooperate, we'll protect you, no one will harm a hair on your head, we'll send you to another country if necessary, you'll have a home, food, money, a car, everything you need to live, on the condition that you give us the names of your contacts. Do they work at *The Tribune*, too?"

"Believe me, sir, I know absolutely nothing about arms traffic!" I begged, *"The Tribune* is only a small newspaper that serves the community..."

The man pounded the desk with his fist again. This time the impact knocked over the ashtray, spilling its contents on the floor. "This old man doesn't want to cooperate! Take him away! Later we'll get the truth out of him, one way or another. The third time's the charm..."

260,000 PEOPLE MARCH THROUGH SAN SAL-
VADOR IN ANTI-GOVERNMENT PROTEST ORGA-
NIZED BY THE COALITION OF REVOLUTIONARY
PARTIES. SOME 20,000 PROTEST PARTICIPANTS DIS-
PERSED BY GOVERNMENT TROOPS TAKE REFUGE
IN THE NATIONAL UNIVERSITY. COFFEE GROWERS
COMBAT NATIONALIZATION OF COFFEE PRODUC-
TION.

Monsignor Romero: I comment: "From the humble comes the light." The government project on which we are commenting, if it wants to save itself, must amputate as soon as possible and without pity the rotten part and keep only the healthy part. A project that through fear or because of certain considerations wants to continue covering up what cannot be covered up is destined for ruin; it will not find stability in the people.

And I am going to refer, thirdly, to the popular project. I look with hope upon the efforts at coordination, above all because they are accompanied by an invitation to the other democratic sectors of the country to create with them a wide and powerful unity. I hope that this invitation is sincere, and that those who make it will assume an attitude of openness and flexibility that will permit the planning and joint realization of an economic-political project capable of obtaining majority consensus from the people and of guaranteeing respect for and development of the faith and the Christian values of the people.

The Pope has said that in the matter of political projects, it is necessary to have great respect for the sentiments of the people. And I say it now, applying it to El Salvador, where certain propaganda—often hypocritical anti-Communist propaganda, of course—attributes to certain organizations, mainly to their leaders, the desire to implant among us ideologies which in no way agree with our Christian nature. Therefore, the popular project which is issuing a call for unity must make every effort to keep in mind the development of our faith and the Christian values of our people, and as a representative of the Church I will insist on it always.

To them, to those behind the popular project, I want to say the same thing I say to the government: that words and promises are not enough, especially when they are screamed with frenzy and demagogic meaning. Actions are needed; and on our behalf, as a Pastor, I will be watching to see if these actions demonstrate that the popular organizations are capable of promoting this broad unity I have just described.

To the popular organizations and, above all, to those of a military and guerrilla nature, whatever their name, I say also: cease immediately those acts of violence and terrorism, often senseless, which provoke more violent situations. I tell you what was said at Puebla: that violence only begets new forms of oppression and slavery which are ordinarily more serious than those from which liberation is sought, but, above all, it is an attack on life, which depends only on the Creator. We must stress also that when an ideology appeals to violence, it thereby acknowledges its own insufficiency and weakness.

In light of these criteria, I must point out the violent acts and events that the Church laments and suffers and with whose victims it is in solidarity.

El Rosario Church, San José Externado, the Cathedral, and other churches in other towns have been taken over. I believe that I can say of these takeovers the same thing that our radio station YSAX commented regarding the takeover of the Panamanian Embassy by the LP-28. Our station said: "At these moments in which the popular unity seeks international support, this takeover is an unsupported action which in no way benefits the credibility of the popular organizations..." I would say also, with regard to our churches, that at this time when the organizations are calling for the unity of the people, why offend the intimate feelings with which our people enter the temples?... I hope the organizations become mature and do not make a game out of something that is so serious, and that our churches of God be respected, if we truly are with the people and want to defend their rights, the most sacred being the right to enter a church and worship God with the conviction of their souls.

Let us include here also the matter of the kidnappings. These also are violent acts which obstruct the country's peace process. I have a very lovely letter from Don José Antonio Morales, who asks me to thank God for the rescue of his grandson Fidelito who was kidnapped months ago, and he relates the tragedy of which he was the object: "It causes great anguish to know that there are men with hearts capable of making others suffer, as the child tells that he suffered when he was in captivity. He was forced to ingest narcotics, and what made him saddest was when he would hear those individuals say that if we didn't pay the money they demanded, they had to kill him. He says that then he thought about his mother and his father and all of us whom he would never see again. We, on the other hand, suffered the same thing, seeing ourselves completely unable to pay the ransom, and the only hope that sustained us was a miracle of God." And he tells how the miracle of God is achieved when there is faith in prayer. This is a testimony, which I include for you and for me, of that trust we have preached in today's gospel.

I am thankful, in the name of human rights, for the attention that the ERP gave to the request to prolong the deadline for concluding the case of Mr. Jaime Hill Arguello. YSAX commented: "We hope that the ERP will be realistic, since that is what we can ask them above all, and that they will accept the national and international conditions in which their action is framed." I insist upon the urgency of negotiating possible conditions for resolving this distressing situation. The wife and family of Mr. Hill assure that: "To ransom him, they are capable of anything, but they find themselves in an impossible situation. And no one is obliged to do the impossible." They beg earnestly for negotiations that are truly within their reach.

In this same manner the family of Mr. Dunn, ex-Ambassador from South Africa, asks the FPL to facilitate the channels of negotiation to bring an end to that conflict. The family states that the publicity goals the FPL was proposing have already been achieved; and they beg them not to be so intransigent in demanding the impossible, since the family does not have the national support of their country and is in a very precarious economic situation. As for myself, since they had the confidence to choose me as mediator, I beg that those conditions be taken into account and that his release be accelerated.

The other kidnapping cases, which for the sake of brevity I will not mention, also concern me, and I do beg those who are responsible for them to do everything possible so that, by respecting the rights of human beings, we may also deserve from God solutions to our national problems.

Soledad put the keys on the night stand. The room was tiny and damp. Against the wall, which was covered with obscene words and drawings, a dresser of uncertain color stood in the corner opposite the bed. On it was a battered old suitcase which revealed part of a flowered dress. From another of the defaced walls hung a drawing of a saint with incredible blue eyes and blond hair, in whose arms rested a plump, naked, smiling child, holding a globe in his small hands.

"You don't have to get undressed," said Rogelio, noticing that Soledad was beginning to unbutton her red blouse.

"What do you mean?" she replied, visibly upset. "I have to make money; if I don't they punish me."

"Don't worry about that." He took a bill out of his wallet and held it out to her. "Is this enough?"

"Yes," she said, taking the money, not knowing what to do or say.

Both of them were silent. Soledad dropped the bill on the night stand and, still indecisive, asked, "What do you want me to do?"

"Nothing, sit down, relax. Tell me more about your life."

"You don't like me, do you? You don't go to bed with trashy women like me."

"Of course I like you," he said, offering her a cigarette and lighting it for her. "But the truth is that I've never paid for..."

"They force me to do it!" she interrupted, blowing out a furious mouthful of smoke as if her purpose were to hurt the air. "I've never been in love with any man. It's hard to love when life does nothing but mistreat us."

"I understand, believe me I understand you. Life hasn't been a bed of roses for me either. I lost my whole family, too. I guess they met the same fate as yours… Life is so strange… I never thought I would find someone who knew them. What a coincidence to meet you, in a place like this!… What is your son's name?"

"Pedrito," she answered, taking from the suitcase a wallet and from that a photo in which the huge, black, sad eyes of a child stood out. "This is my little son when I left him at the church gate." Immediately her eyes grew wet and she began to kiss the paper as if it were her son himself. "Dear God, I wonder where my son is! Where is he?!" She raised her arms and knelt in front of the picture of the saint, her eyes filled with tears that slid down her cheeks and splashed to the floor. "My God, take care of my Pedrito!"

Rogelio took her gently by the arm and helped her up. He caressed her hair and hugged her tenderly.

"Why don't you escape? Go far away from here! You're young and can make a new life for yourself."

"I've thought about that many times, but I have nowhere to go. This is my home. I don't know anyone outside of here. I don't trust anyone. Besides, don't you understand that no one wants me? I'm garbage. If I had somewhere to go, I would have fled a long time ago."

"You can go to the United States," was the only thing he could think of to say.

"To the United States? How? With whom? Where? If I knew how, I'd go to hell itself, since it couldn't be any worse than this place."

"I know some people that can get you out of the country and help you enter the United States. I lived in New York for several years. I know how to do it. They would help you cross the border and get you a job."

"It's hard to believe," she said, looking at him with an empty and incredulous gaze. "So many lies have made me distrust all men. But I've suffered so much that one more isn't going to hurt me… If you help me, I'm willing to go."

"I'll arrange the trip for you. But don't tell anyone about this. Both of us would be in danger."

"No, no one, I promise you, but help me, please. God will pay you for this, sir. Help me for your own life. I have no way to pay you, only my body. If you help me, you can do anything you want to with me."

"Let's go out now, before they come looking for us. Fix up your face. I'll come back soon to give you news about the trip."

"But don't forget, please," she begged, holding him tightly. "Help me, because I can no longer bear this dog's life that they give me. Look, three days ago I slashed my wrists. I was willing to take my own life," she said, showing him her forearms with still-bloody scars. "But even in killing myself I have bad luck. When they found me, they tied me to a chair and locked me in a dark room without food for two days. Please don't forget me. God will repay you."

"Don't worry," he said, squeezing her icy hands and caressing her wet cheeks. "Everything will work out fine. I promise you. In a couple of weeks you'll be out of here."

"What the hell, Rogelio," said Domínguez when he saw them return to the Red Room. "You sure squeezed all the juice out of the poor girl. Don't be a glutton, man."

"We're going to sleep now," said Chata.

The two women picked up the glasses and empty bottles from the table and left.

"Three o'clock in the morning," said Domínguez, not even surprised. "We'd better get going, too."

Several taxis were waiting out on the dark, rainy street. They got into the first one.

"This is a true oasis. Right, Rogelio?"

"So it seems," he said, leaning back. Soledad's anguished face and Pedrito's huge, sad eyes persisted in his mind. "So it seems."

THREE CHRISTIAN DEMOCRATS JOIN GOVERN-MENT JUNTA. LP-28 MILITANTS OCCUPY PANA-MANIAN EMBASSY AND TAKE AMBASSADORS FROM PANAMA AND COSTA RICA HOSTAGE. REBEL FORCES INVADE SAN SALVADOR NEIGHBOR-HOODS; TWO SOLDIERS DIE IN THE FIGHTING.

Monsignor Romero: Above all, I want to congratulate you because you give to this moment the true identity of God's people. I refer to a comment that a Venezuelan politician who was with us, having come with a certain curiosity, made to me last Sunday. He had been told that our masses were really political meetings and that people came out of political curiosity; this was a serious mischaracterization of our Sunday Mass.

Besides being a politician, this man is a great Christian, and he said to me: "Now I realize that this is a true Christian assembly because the people sing, pray and, above all, when the moment of communion arrived, the great procession of people that approached the Eucharist impressed me tremendously." I felt a very intense joy, because what I am trying to achieve has nothing to do with politics.

If, because of the necessity of the moment, I am illuminating the politics of my country, it is as a pastor, it is from the Gospel, it is a light that has the obligation to illuminate the country's paths and contribute as a Church what the Church has to give. Therefore I ask that we give this gathering all the identifying marks of a community of God, which by its very nature exists in the midst of the natural community, the country, and feels the responsibility of meditating on the Gospel in order to then be, each of us in his own surroundings, a multiplier of this word, an illuminator of the country's paths.

The circumstances are entirely appropriate. And what circumstance isn't if the Gospel is an incarnation of God in all human circumstances? At this moment when the country is living in fear, confusion and uncertainty, how much we need a word of serenity, of infinite reach: the Gospel!

From this Church that should be the light of the world, it is precisely toward the world around us that we look to try to illumine it with faith. When I expressed in Louvain the political dimension of the faith, I finished by saying that what marks the limits of this political dimension of the faith for our Church is precisely the world of the poor. In the diversity of political opportunities, what matters to us is poor people. I do not wish to detail for you all the fluctuations of politics in my country; I have preferred to explain to you the deep roots of the Church's actions in this explosive world of Salvadoran socio-politics, and I have tried to clarify for you the ultimate criterion, which is theological and historical, for the actions of the Church in this field: the world of the poor. According to how they, the poor, are affected, the Church will support, specifically as the Church, one political project or another. That is, this is how the Church sees things at this moment of the homily: to support what benefits the poor...as well as to denounce all that is evil for the people. By this criterion, let us judge some of this week's events. For example:

The notorious Decree 114 was promulgated, which has provoked so many arguments. The Church is not interested in the legalisms which often mask selfishness. The Church is interested in whether this decree is truly going to be a free step toward the transformations that the poor need, or whether it will not be an efficient path toward that point. If it means something good for the poor, the Church is in agreement; and if it means nothing to the poor, the decree does not interest the Church either.

Lamentably, in spite of that open path, the promises continue to be unfulfilled in deeds. What has been most evident this week is that neither the Junta, nor the Christian Democratic Party, is governing the country. They are only allowing themselves to be used to give this appearance at the national and international levels. The February 12 massacre of demonstrating members of MERS and the bloody eviction of the occupants of the headquarters of the Christian Democratic Party show clearly that it is not they who govern; rather it is the most repressive sector of the Armed Forces and the security forces that does. The very leaders of the Christian Democratic Party recognized that these acts can be considered nothing less than disobedience and contravention of the position adopted by the Junta through Colonel Majano, when nonintervention of the security forces was assured. It did not matter to those people that a daughter of a member of the Junta was there, as well as the wife of the Minister of Education; much less did they care about respecting the lives of the occupants. They assassinated, they brutally assassinated, several of them. The descriptions that have come to us through eyewitnesses are horrifying.

If the Junta and the Christian Democratic Party do not wish to be accomplices to so much abuse of power and so many crimes, they must identify and sanction those responsible. It is not enough to say they are going to investigate. There are eyewitnesses, worthy of credibility in the opinion of members of the Junta and the Party, who can shorten the investigation. Also, the families of those assassinated are still waiting to be indemnified by the Security Forces. In this way the hopes that those responsible for the repression of previous regimes will be sanctioned are becoming more and more distant, seeing that the current military authorities and members of the Security Forces, like their predecessors, continue staining their hands with blood because they continue to repress the people now more than ever.

With this also it has been shown that the current government lacks popular support; it relies only on the Armed Forces and the support of some foreign powers. This is another serious responsibility of the Christian Democratic Party: that its presence in the government, together with private political and economic interests, is moving countries like Venezuela and the United States to support an alternative which claims to be anti-oligarchic but in truth is anti-popular...

Domínguez: One man went to open the door and another indicated to me that I should get up and walk. We again travelled through the hallways, but this time we went down to the basement. They opened an iron door and, suddenly, an overpowering stench filled my lungs. I shuddered, thinking that soon my body would begin to decompose and become part of that pestilence. They closed the door and pushed me along. In the darkness, I began to make out bars of cells and motionless and shapeless forms that moaned and cried out, delirious. With a shove they pushed me into a cell. The bars closed with a scream of rusted metal that echoed sharply. The clicking of the men's footsteps faded. The basement door opened and slammed shut, leaving everything completely dark... and silent. The foul smell had contaminated the air and I felt like I was fainting. Resting my head against the wall, I slid toward the floor and, when I tried to sit down, I made contact with a soft object, almost like a pillow, and I rested my head there. My exhaustion, the lack of ventilation, and my confusion and uncertainty added to my resignation and, lulled by a weak voice attempting to sing in a neighboring cell, I began to fall asleep as if I were under the effect of a powerful drug... "Fly... Fly...little bird, fly...fly to...your nest, because here...ends the story...of one who...died...for his party..."

That sad voice was the prelude to a nightmare... Several men took me to a room from whose walls hung hoods, whips, strange devices. In one corner, an iron cot without a mattress, two chairs and a wooden table. "This is where we bring those who don't want to confess willingly, and we have to use force," said one of the men. "We tie them to the cot, connect wires to their ears and give them electric shocks that shake their bodies and cause great pain..." Another added: "And there's the hood that we never hesitate to use. We fill it with quicklime and pull it down over your head. It burns your eyes and stops your breathing. You feel like you're drowning. Then we tie you by your testicles and hang you from the ceiling. And if you still don't tell the truth, we cut out your eyes and inject you with drugs that will make you confess anything..." The mere mention of such tortures left me horrified. My strength failed me and, when I was going to collapse on the floor, one of the men grabbed me by the arm. "Don't worry, old man, don't die on us too soon. Your turn will come, and then we'll see what you're made of..."

I don't know how long I was asleep, but I awoke with a start as I was grabbed by the arms and pulled to my feet. A man standing at the entrance to the cell shined a bright light on me which also illuminated the object I had used as a pillow. It was a dead body. One of the men said, "this idiot died; better clean the cell." We again passed through the foul-smelling corridors and climbed the dirty stairway until we found ourselves back in the upstairs hallways with other escorted prisoners. We went to the same office and they sat me down on the same bench.

This is it, I thought. They're serious this time. They'll interrogate me again, and they'll threaten me; they don't realize that I'm resigned to my fate. The memory of the prisoner's song came to me and I was filled with sadness, which disappeared with the chills I felt remembering the torture chamber that appeared in my nightmare.

The interrogator came close to me, lighting one cigarette with the butt of another. "You've been saved by the bell, old man," he said. "You're lucky that several influential ministers interceded on your behalf... They've saved your skin..."

Those words caused me great surprise, creating in me a sudden and deep joy for life. "From now on behave yourself, you little bastard," he continued, in the same crude tone of voice which somehow no longer repulsed me. "The next time will be the last, fool. We'll be keeping a close eye on you; one wrong move and that's it, you're screwed, it won't matter if a hundred ministers intercede for you... Take this old man to the nurse's station so they can patch him up. They'll be coming for him soon."

And I felt like a child again, Rogelio. As if I had just been born after being imprisoned for centuries in the womb of a horrible nightmare.

San Salvador, February 17, 1980

President of the
United States of America
Jimmy Carter

Mr. President:

Recently a news item has appeared in the national press that has concerned me greatly. According to the report, your government is considering the possibility of supporting and assisting, economically and militarily, the Government Junta.

Because you are a Christian, and because you have indicated that you wish to defend human rights, I dare express to you my pastoral point of view concerning this news report, and to make a concrete request of you.

The news that the United States government is considering supporting the arms race in El Salvador by sending military equipment and advisers to "train three Salvadoran battalions in logistics, communications and intelligence" worries me deeply. If this information in the news is true, your government's contribution, rather than promoting greater justice and peace in El Salvador, will undoubtedly worsen the injustice and repression against the organized people, who often have been struggling for their most fundamental human rights to be respected.

The present Government Junta and especially the Armed Forces and security forces unfortunately have not demonstrated their capacity to resolve, politically and structurally, our grave national problems. In general they have only resorted to repressive violence, producing a toll of dead and wounded much greater than the military regimes of the recent past, whose systematic violation of human rights was denounced by none other than the Inter-American Human Rights Commission.

The brutal manner in which the security forces recently removed and assassinated occupants of the headquarters of the Christian Democratic Party, although the Government Junta and the Party—it seems—did not authorize said operation, is evidence that the Junta and the Christian Democratic Party do not govern the country, but rather that political power is in the hands of unscrupulous members of the military who know only how to repress the people and favor the interests of the Salvadoran oligarchy.

If it is true that last November "a group of six Americans was in El Salvador supplying two hundred thousand dollars in gas masks and protective vests and providing training regarding their use against demonstrations," you must be informed that it is evident that from then on the security forces, with greater personal protection and efficiency, have repressed the people even more violently, using deadly weapons.

Therefore, given that as a Salvadoran and as Archbishop of the Archdiocese of San Salvador I have the obligation to see that faith and justice reign in my country, I ask, if you truly want to defend human rights, that you:

Prohibit the giving of military aid to the Salvadoran Government.

Guarantee that your government will not intervene, directly or indirectly, with military, economic, or diplomatic pressure, in determining the destiny of the Salvadoran people.

At this moment we are experiencing a grave economic-political crisis in our country, but it is undeniable that the people are the ones who have been growing in political consciousness and organizing themselves more and more, and thereby have begun to equip themselves to be the negotiators and to be responsible for the future of El Salvador, and the only ones able to overcome the crisis.

It would be unjust and deplorable if, because of the intervention of foreign powers, the Salvadoran people were thwarted, repressed, and prevented from freely deciding with autonomy the economic and political trajectory that our country should follow.

It would constitute a violation of a right that we Latin-American bishops gathered in Puebla recognized publicly when we said: "the legitimate self-determination of our peoples that permits them to organize according to their own will and the march of their history and to cooperate in a new international order." (Puebla, 505).

I hope that your religious sentiments and your sensitivity to the defense of human rights will move you to accept my petition, thereby avoiding greater bloodshed in this suffering country.

Very truly yours,
Oscar Arnulfo Romero, Archbishop

The weekend at my parents' house with Rogelio was truly pleasant; it made us forget the violence of San Salvador for a couple of days. Unfortunately, Sunday afternoon descended on the high plateau of Ilobasco and forced us to bid farewell to my parents, who urged Rogelio to return soon, assuring him that the house was at his disposal and that he would always be received with open arms.

We boarded the bus to the capital. As the vehicle drove away, I watched through the window as the distance shrunk the silhouettes of my parents and brother who, with their persistent waving, were saying goodbye as if it were for the last time, as if we were travelling toward a strange and unpredictable land.

The first part of the return to San Salvador went by in silence. I remember that I wrote down in my notebook certain metaphors that occurred to me, thinking that perhaps, with luck, they would become poems. Then I began to study the other passengers. Among them a large number of dark-skinned, serious and silent men, possibly laborers or peasants, stood out. The women never took their eyes off their baskets of fruit, fresh cheese and bottles of cream. Some children were sleeping on their mothers' laps and others, their eyes glued to the windows, observed the villages and light posts that were going by rapidly.

Rogelio was quiet and pensive, but it was he who finally broke the silence with a comment about the kindness of my family. I responded that they were all I had in this world and that they meant very much to me…

"They keep my spirits up. They give me the courage to face life. I don't know what I would do without them."

"You're very lucky," said Rogelio. "I'm all alone, since my whole family, as you know, disappeared during the border problems with Honduras."

"How sad," I said. "How is it possible that such small, poor countries, instead of working together for a united Central America, wage war against each other? When will we realize that we have a common history, culture, tradition and destiny, that we are blood brothers, that since the time of the Spanish conquest we have suffered the same fate?

Suddenly the bus stopped abruptly. The brakes squealed and the passengers screamed, falling to the floor among suitcases and baskets, fruit and chickens, pieces of cheese and bottles of cream that rolled under the seats, breaking against the walls of the bus. I managed to grab hold of Rogelio, who instinctively had grasped the bars of the seat in front of us to avoid falling to the floor.

The driver shouted: "There are bodies in the middle of the road! I can't drive over them!"

The driver's assistant was helping a woman who was still buried under baskets of fruit and bread.

"We have to move them! Help us!" called the driver. "There are several!"

His assistant gestured to Rogelio. "You, sir, help us move them; hurry!"

Several men got out and, with the light from the bus headlights and some flashlights, located four bodies. "Let's go! Quick!"

The driver and a passenger picked up one body and carried it to the side of the road. I got out also, to offer my help. Rogelio asked me to go back to my seat but, realizing my determination, gave in. The cadavers were those of National Guardsmen, now destroyed by the many vehicles that had run over them, without stopping to remove them from the road.

"Let's move this one," said the assistant, lifting the arms of one of the dead men.

I grabbed one of the feet, Rogelio took the other, and we dragged the body over to the grass. The strong headlights of the bus clearly illuminated the man's face. When I saw him, I could not hide my surprise. It was the agent who had checked our identification cards on Saturday. Rogelio recognized him too. It was the same man who had insisted that Rogelio paint his portrait, whom Rogelio had planned to visit to try to find out about the fate of Ignacio, whom the Guardsman seemed to know. But now there he was, frozen, his eyes unfocused, his open mouth revealing a purple tongue and a few gold-crowned teeth, and his forehead spattered with dried blood around several bullet holes.

"Hurry, please!" begged the assistant, covering his nose with a handkerchief and pushing Rogelio and me toward the bus. "Let's go!"

The driver was already at the wheel.

"Let's get out of here!" he shouted, pushing the accelerator to the floor, as if the bus were being pursued by the devil himself.

"Poor Guardsmen," said one woman. "Nowadays no one is safe."

Rogelio offered me a handkerchief so I could wipe my hands.

"How horrible!" I said, when I saw it stained with blood, unable to erase from my mind the diabolical expression on the disfigured face of the dead Guardsman.

FPL MILITANTS ATTACK NATIONAL GUARD HEAD-
QUARTERS WITH ANTI-TANK BOMBS. NATIONAL
GUARD DEPLOYS TANKS THROUGHOUT THE CITY.
29 DEAD AND 14 WOUNDED.

Editorial office. Rogelio is concentrating on his work. He seems to pay no attention to the movements of Domínguez, who paces the office nervously, smoking, furiously blowing mouthfuls of smoke. Domínguez puts out his cigarette in the ashtray. He goes to the window and contemplates the city.

Domínguez: We're really screwed, Rogelio. It makes you feel like packing your bags and getting the hell out. Staying here is like waiting to be decapitated. You don't know exactly when it's your turn, but you sense that it's soon, very soon... The city is being destroyed; it's collapsing. Look at that corner (he points), the sidewalks stained with blood, the walls full of dark words.

(Rogelio gets up and goes to the window.)

Domínguez: Look what that one says: "Yesterday Cuba, today Nicaragua, tomorrow El Salvador."

Rogelio (returning to his desk): There are many people who want nothing to do with the left or the right; the only thing that matters to them is to work and get on with their lives. They aren't interested in politics.

Domínguez: But they can't escape this situation either. They end up dead anyway. Even the innocent are swept up in this storm of violence.

(Moncada, the administrator, appears in the doorway.)

Domínguez: Hello, Moncada, come in. How can we help you?

Moncada (enters the office): I'm very sorry, Domínguez, but I bring you some very bad news.

Domínguez (goes toward the chair behind his desk): What is it, Moncada? Let me have it. Don't hide anything.

Moncada (hands a paper to Domínguez): Look. This note was given to the secretary by a stranger. It's a double threat. Death to the director if he doesn't leave the country immediately and, also, a threat to blow up the newspaper office if we don't close it.

Domínguez (in a scornful tone, trying to downplay the seriousness of the threat): It's not the first time.

Moncada: I know very well that it's not the first, but now the employees are more worried than ever. Some have already gone home. Others are afraid to come to work. I really don't know what to do.

Rogelio (looking at the note): What happened with the last threat?

Moncada: The truth, Rogelio, is that this is the third threat, isn't that right, Domínguez?

Domínguez: Yes. The first time, the director left the country, stayed away for several months, and nothing happened. (Domínguez paces across the office, under the intense gaze of Moncada and Rogelio.) The second time they planted a bomb and the terrorists telephoned threatening the director with death so that he would close down the paper. When he didn't comply, they kidnapped him. They freed him after a time.

Moncada (to Domínguez): And we mustn't forget the incident of your arrest, which you survived only by a miracle.

Domínguez (avoiding the subject of his arrest): Any news about the photographer and the reporter?

Moncada: No, they haven't been seen for two days. I hope nothing has happened to them.

Domínguez: Maybe they just got drunk and went on a binge like last month. Remember we had to go pick them up at Majagual Beach? They had pawned even the cameras...

Rogelio: What do you think the reason for this latest threat is?

Domínguez: Who knows? It could well be because of the series of articles and photographs on human rights abuses that we've been publishing. It so happens that the two men who are missing were the ones in charge of those stories.

Monsignor Romero: I ask the Christian Democratic Party to analyze not only its intentions, which of course may be very good, but also the real effects its presence is causing. Its presence is covering up, especially at the international level, the repressive nature of the current regime. It is urgent that as a political force of our people, it find the way to most effectively utilize that force on behalf of our poor: whether isolated and powerless, in a government controlled by a repressive military, or as one more force that joins a broad project of the popular government, whose base of support is not the current Armed Forces, which are ever more corrupt, but rather the majority consensus of our people.

I am not opposed to the institution of the Armed Forces.

I continue to believe that there are honest elements in it that are the hope of its own recovery. I also believe in the need for true security forces to protect our people. Nevertheless, I cannot agree with those members of the military who, abusing their rank, are causing the loss of prestige of these necessary institutions, converting them into instruments of repression and injustice. This gives the impression that the right wing is governing... And so it will continue, as long as the government does not identify and punish those who are responsible for so much repression and as long as it is incapable of carrying out the reforms proposed on behalf of the poor, because it is the oligarchy that is taking advantage of this political weakness of the government to attack it and prevent it, by military force, from carrying out its reforms.

The popular rumor about the conspiracy between the security forces and the clandestine armed right wing groups is being heard more and more. The suffering of the people has grown so much that recounting the violent acts by the right wing has become impossible. Only as an example, I want to refer to my beloved priests. Because just as fertilizer, manure, makes gardens more beautiful, so too the calumny of these days has made the holiness of our apostles in the pastoral fields flower. Here we have some very beautiful letters from priests who repudiate the calumny and make its authors responsible for what may happen to them. And they ratify their commitment to the people, because they are committed to no one other than to Christ and to the people who reflect the holiness of Christ our Lord.

Among these letters, which would be too many to enumerate, I have also received information about the machine-gunning of the residence of the Jesuit Fathers. On Saturday February 16 at 12:45 in the morning, bursts of G-3 and machine-gun fire were heard. Some 100 bullet holes were found in the outer doors of the house, in the two inside floors and in a car. After the shooting, a car was heard speeding away. The Jesuits who in recent years have been persecuted live in this residency. We should remember the 1973 prosecution for the matters of San José School, the assassination of Jesuit Father Grande and other similar facts which demonstrate how this priestly order is hated and persecuted as we have said before, because of their commitment to the people.

In addition, 52 Jesuits who work in Guatemala have been threatened in reaction to the document they wrote, on behalf of all the Jesuits of Central America, to denounce the systematic abuse of power, economic injustice, and the increase of indiscriminate violence and the serious violations of the human rights of the indigenous population in Guatemala.

Our magazine, Búsqueda, which I recommend to you highly, contains an article about Father Rafael Palacios, who was assassinated on June 20 of last year, and about Father José Alirio Napoleón Macías, assassinated August 4. Documents, testimonies and writings have been gathered which reflect that these priests are far from being Communist infiltrators and indeed are true messengers of the gospel of Jesus Christ.

I also have received an extremely sad letter from Juan Alcides Guardado, who was on his way to his home in Caserío El Picacho, Cantón La Laguna, Las Vueltas, Chalatenango. And when he was on the way, he was told not to continue, that it all had been decimated, and truly, he was unable to find even his own mother. He asks that I, by means of this radio broadcast, make this announcement to ask his mother to give some indication of where she is so that he may go to find her. What absurd things happen in our fatherland!

Many of those who have taken refuge in the Cathedral are from there, as I said, and many are still fleeing from this wave of terrorism.

A letter from Mrs. María Ignacia Rivera, from San Agustín in Usulután, also cries out denouncing the assassination of her son Manuel de Jesús. He leaves his wife widowed with six small children.

Professor Agustín Osmín Hernández, was captured by five security agents on February 12 at 1:30 in the morning in Aguilares. His wife and the community of Zacamil are concerned about him. May this notice serve to speed his release or place him before the courts, as is just.

Testimonies of solidarity regarding the machine-gunning of the home of Professor Guillermo Galvin have also arrived.

Dr. Roberto Lara Velado has received death threats. Those of us who are acquainted with his honorable career can do nothing less than be in solidarity with him and denounce these death threats against the honorable and Christian person of Dr. Roberto Lara Velado.

The most serious matter is that the extreme right is plotting a military coup. This is being talked about a lot. So also is a general strike of private businesses. It would be unforgivable to suppress the march of our people's aspiration for justice. Those who support the unjust order in which we live in no way have the right to initiate an insurrection, but a victory of this sort over a people that has already achieved political consciousness would cost a great deal of blood and would not succeed in drowning the people's clamor for justice. The most logical course is for the powerful members of the oligarchy to reflect with human or Christian serenity, if possible, upon the call that Christ makes to them today from the Gospel: "Woe be to you, for tomorrow you will weep!" It is best, repeating the well-known image, to take off your rings before they cut off your hand. Be logical with your human and Christian convictions, and give the people a chance to organize with a sense of justice; do not attempt to defend what cannot be defended...

My hands nervously gripping my brushes, I faced the piece of paper spread on my drawing table. I wanted to paint a landscape, perhaps a silhouette at a window watching the sun set. But the view from my window did not lend itself to what I intended. At other times it had provided beautiful shapes and vibrant colors. But now it too had been vandalized by the struggle, by the war between the man who persisted in his domination and the one who had decided to abolish it. The war violated the landscape. It turned it into a forum where gladiators and wild beasts, fury and blood confronted each other day and night.

Nevertheless, driven by my stubborn desire to create, I worked on the painting until I finished it. The piece showed struggle, pain, death. The mountain in the background was covered not with flowers, but with crosses. Nor was it green as before. Nor blue as on the best days. Against my will, the color red predominated. Blood red! The sky in the painting was dark gray, not blue. The sun had grown dark. It radiated darkness. It reflected not life but death.

"Simón's right," I said to Lourdes. "These paintings are horrible."

"But they depict the true panorama," she said, observing the composition. "Though depressing, it's honest. As an artist, your duty is to observe and document, to be a witness to history, to mold reality in your art so that it becomes a testimony to the human task."

"But this piece lacks the least bit of fantasy," I said sadly. "And no matter how objective it aspires to be, art shouldn't border on realism. The artist must add his own poetry, create a work that transcends reality. Otherwise art offers nothing new; it limits itself; it says nothing different. It becomes photography, the instrument of dogma. Personal feelings are completely excluded."

"Whether you intend it or not, your artistic sentiments are always reflected in your work, because even this painting, which you find dismal and depressing, reflects reality's oppression of your very creativity. It demonstrates the fact that art also suffers from the violence in which we live."

"But then where is the hope with which art supposedly comforts humanity, that lets humankind escape its cruel reality? Where's the illusion?"

"That's absurd," argued Lourdes scornfully. "If you consider yourself an honest artist, how can you paint beautiful pictures while out in the street people are being killed for demanding their most fundamental rights, like the right to live? Art needn't be beautiful, but pure. And art that comes close to this purity, that truly reflects our present life, is what you've just painted."

Seized by frustration, I grabbed the painting and tore it into countless fragments, and began throwing them into a corner where failed attempts from other days and nights had accumulated—attempts at free and spontaneous creativity devoured by reality.

"Even those torn and destroyed paintings," continued Lourdes in the face of my desperation, "document the art and times of today. And there's absolutely nothing conflictive about it. Conflict appears when we refuse to accept the reality from which neither we nor art itself can escape, since both suffer the same fate."

And from the moment that Lourdes' words identified the crisis my painting was going through, the fantasy of my prior works was destroyed. It was as if the characters became embarrassed by their strictly decorative function; the colors darkened and the shapes deflated.

One Sunday, after listening to Monsignor Romero's homily on the radio, I enthusiastically showed Lourdes a picture I had painted the night before, a composition that reflected no ambition other than pure and free creativity: an abstract painting.

"The silence and indifference of this painting, in light of the current situation, make it an accomplice of the repressive system," was her reaction after a brief examination.

"But art only obeys art," I said, infuriated, frustrated at such rejection of my artistic zeal. "Art can't always let itself be carried away by reality, because it's a phenomenon that makes its own laws, based on the sacred principle of free expression. Free of dogmas, space and time, transcending the world's problems and establishing itself as a symbol of pure creativity."

"You talk like a perfect bourgeois, insensitive to the suffering of your race. Where is the humanistic sentiment of art?"

And my painting, the life raft which until then had saved me from sinking into chaos, was abruptly capsizing. Its magic and enchantment were disappearing. The rich elements in fantastic allegories were becoming empty, sterile, colorless. But I also understood that now, more than ever, I needed to create, to paint. It was the only way to avoid being carried away by the violence, and thereby fueling it. But the conflict between art and reality was causing me an asphyxiating desperation, since I was not sure if my painting should portray reality's oppression of creativity, or the unjust reality that was oppressing the people. Or perhaps I needed a painting that would show both types of oppression.

"What should I do, Lourdes, as an artist in the midst of this disaster? What road should I take?"

"Maybe these words of Ernesto Sábato will help you," Lourdes said, taking out a paper which she read aloud: "In the midst of disaster and combat, immersed in a reality which quakes and collapses all along enormous fissures, artists are divided between those who bravely confront the chaos, creating literature"—a work of art, she remarked, to generalize— "that describes man's condition in decline; and those that, fearing the revulsion, withdraw to their ivory towers or retreat to worlds of fantasy."

That same night I covered several old paintings with white paint, and in long vigils filled with passion and rage, I painted a series of compositions entitled "Liberation." The new pictures showed people shouting, demanding a stop to the repression, violence, persecution, torture, hunger and poverty. The paintings were filled with malnourished children, assassinated peasants and workers, anguished and ragged mothers. The figure of Monsignor Romero appeared, denouncing massacres. But things continued the same, if not worse, in the street as well as in my distressed spirit. All that indignation and protest on my canvas changed nothing. Newly frustrated, I confessed to Lourdes my decision to stop painting.

"The celestial metaphor cannot put on airs and turn its beautiful back on the woman and children crying next to the cadaver of their loved one. Impossible. Art for its own sake has no reason to exist."

"Don't be discouraged, Rogelio. If you're a true artist you'll return to your brushes. What's happening is that your artistic and moral convictions are in conflict; they're going through an important crisis. And if they survive, you'll begin again with new conviction, and a new way of looking at things, at the world, that will forge the way for a new style of painting that reflects your circumstances. Because that's art: circumstance and conviction, conscience and determination. Life. The rest doesn't matter; it's excess.

JUNTA MEMBER AND CABINET OFFICIAL RESIGN "IN PROTEST AGAINST GOVERNMENT POLITICS OF REFORMS WITH REPRESSION."

Editor's office. Moncada, the administrator, pushes the door open. Domínguez and Rogelio greet him. He carries a handful of papers in one hand and photographs in the other. His face appears serious, his hair uncombed. He gives the impression of being extremely upset.

Moncada: With your permission.

Domínguez: Come in, how can we help you?

Moncada: Now we're screwed. The bodies of the reporter and the photographer have been found. Several panic-stricken employees have resigned. Now we'll have to close down the paper for sure. Here is the report about the two victims, just look how awful. (He hands notes and photographs to Domínguez).

Domínguez: How dreadful! How is it possible for a human being to take another's life in such a savage way?

Moncada: An act of infernal beasts.

Rogelio: (looks at the pictures and is shaken by an intense shiver): My God... They've cut them into pieces.

Moncada: According to the reports, first they tortured them, then they shot them in the face and the chest. Afterward they mutilated their hands and legs, cutting them into several pieces, and finally they cut off their genitals.

Domínguez: A true butchering.

Moncada: And as if all that weren't enough, the threats to dynamite the office continue. (He pauses and looks Domínguez directly in the eye.) I think the best thing to do is to close down the paper. I don't believe it's fair to expose the lives of our employees to the danger that continuing to publish *The Tribune* would mean.

Domínguez: And what do the employees think?

Moncada: The majority of them want to continue. Mainly to avoid losing their jobs. It's not an ideological position. It's simply a matter of survival.

Domínguez (approaches the administrator and returns the reports to him): How many employees are left?

Moncada: Enough for production. There are still dedicated people... The director is in Europe. We established communication with him. He said that for reasons of personal security he will remain outside the country for a time and that, meanwhile, we should elect an interim director. I can't handle the position. I only know about administering funds and distribution. The only one here with the right experience is you, Domínguez. All the administrators have agreed that we want to ask you to assume the director's position. (He puts a hand on Domínguez' shoulder.) What do you say? Do you accept?

Domínguez: I don't know what to tell you, Moncada. You've taken me by surprise. I think that accepting the job would put my own life in danger, and that is serious indeed. Remember, they've already arrested me once and I survived only by a miracle.

Moncada: Certainly. The situation is very serious. A matter of life and death. Therefore think it over, and give me your answer tomorrow... Excuse me now, I should return to my office; I'm sure they need me there. I'll see you later. (He leaves the office and closes the door.)

Domínguez (approaching Rogelio): What do you advise me to do, Rogelio? Should I take the job or not? How do you see the situation?

Rogelio: Don't ask me. You already know that I'm indecisive about everything. I don't know what to do with my own life, much less advise others.

Domínguez (insisting): At least give me an opinion. You must have something to say about it. Besides, don't pretend to be so indecisive because you know very well you're not. Especially in critical situations, like in the case of the girl from the Red Light.

Rogelio: Soledad's case was very different. I had to help her at all costs, without thinking it over much. She was on the verge of suicide, alone and abandoned. Luckily she was able to escape.

Domínguez: You see? And I, what should I do? At least give me your opinion.

Rogelio: The way I look at it, the situation is this. If you don't take over, the paper closes down and many people will be left unemployed. And besides, the closing will be another victory for the oppressors of human rights. *The Tribune* will be cast into oblivion. On the other hand, if you accept and the paper continues to function, it's possible that they'll bomb us and that more employees, including yourself, will die, but in the meantime *The Tribune* will continue, as Lourdes would say: "Like a beacon of light, of hope, in the midst of a tumultuous sea."

Domínguez (walking away from his desk toward the window): Very poetic, but that's all. It's not exactly an optimistic picture.

Rogelio: That's right. Dark from any angle. That's why the decision should be yours and yours alone...

Domínguez (suddenly agitated): This is nonsense, Rogelio! Give me the phone; we're going to take care of this right now! (He dials and waits a few seconds.) Moncada? This is Domínguez. I've decided. I accept the job...and its consequences. (Domínguez realizes that rarely in his life, perhaps never, has he experienced this sudden sensation of self confidence. Rogelio watches him, deeply moved.) But listen, Moncada; this time things will be done my way, understand?

Monsignor Romero: And now I invite you to see, from this Church which tries to be the Kingdom of God on earth and therefore must illuminate the realities of our surroundings.

We have experienced a tremendously tragic week.

I was not able to give you information about last Saturday, March 15, but one of the harshest and most painful military operations in the peasant zones was carried out that day. The affected cantons were La Laguna, Plan de Ocotes, and El Rosario, and a tragic toll resulted from the operations. Many burned farms, plundering, and as always, deaths. In La Laguna, Ernesto Navas, his wife Audelia Mejía de Navas, and their children Martín and Hilda, ages 13 and 7, were killed, along with 11 other peasants.

We also have, without names: in Plan de Ocotes, four peasant farmers and two children; two women in El Rosario; and three other peasants. This was on Saturday.

On Sunday, one week ago, in Arcatao, peasant farmers Vicente Ayala, age 24, his son Freddy, and Marcelino Serrano were assassinated by four members of ORDEN. That same day in Canton Calera of Jutiapa, peasant Fernando Hernández Navarro was assassinated as he fled from a military operation.

March 17 was a terribly violent day. That was last Monday. Several bombs exploded in the capital and in the interior of the country. At the headquarters of the Ministry of Agriculture the damages were very considerable.

The National University campus was besieged by the military from early in the morning until 7 p.m. All day machine-gun fire was heard in the area of the university. The Archbishop's office intervened to protect the persons who were inside.

Eighteen people died in Hacienda Colima: at least 15 of them were peasants. The administrator and owner of the hacienda were also killed. The Armed Forces report that it was a battle. The scene was shown on television and there were many interesting analyses.

At least 50 people died in the grave events of this day. In the capital, seven persons in the incidents in Colonia Santa Lucía. Near Tecnillantas, five persons. In the garbage-collection section, after the evacuation of that institution by the military, the bodies of four workers captured in that action were found.

At kilometer 38 of the highway to Suchitoto in Cantón Montepeque, 16 peasants died. That same day, in Tecnillantas, two UCA students, two brothers, Mario Nelson and Miguel Alberto Rodríguez Velado, were captured. The first was turned over to the courts after four days of illegal detention, but not so his brother, who was wounded and is still in illegal detention. Legal Aid has intervened in his defense.

Amnesty International issued a press release in which it described the repression of the peasants, especially in the area of Chalatenango.

The week's news confirms this report although the government denied it. As I was entering the church, I was given a cable which says: "Amnesty International ratified today"—yesterday—"that in El Salvador human rights are being violated to extremes that have not been seen in other countries." This declaration was made by Patricio Fuentes, spokesman for the special-action project for Central America of the Amnesty Section in Sweden, in an interview in Managua.

Fuentes declared that during two weeks of investigations that he carried out in El Salvador, he was able to confirm the occurrence of 83 political assassinations between March 10 and March 14. He pointed out that Amnesty International recently condemned the government of El Salvador, declaring it responsible for 600 political assassinations... The Salvadoran government in turn defended itself against the charges, arguing that Amnesty had condemned it on the basis of suppositions. "Now we have proven that in El Salvador human rights are violated to an extent worse than the repression that occurred in Chile following the coup," said Fuentes... The Salvadoran government also said that the 600 dead were the result of armed confrontations between Army troops and guerrillas. Fuentes said that during his stay in El Salvador, he was able to see that the victims had been tortured before being assassinated.

The Amnesty spokesman said that the bodies of the victims characteristically appear with their thumbs tied behind their backs. Corrosive liquids were also applied to the bodies to avoid identification of the victims by their relatives, in order to make international denunciations difficult, he added. Nevertheless, the dead have been identified after exhumation. Fuentes said that the repression by the Salvadoran Army has as its goal the dismantling of the popular organizations through the assassination of leaders in the city as well as in the country.

Editor's Office. A few minutes after Domínguez accepted the position, the news had spread through all the offices of the newspaper. Photographers, reporters, typists, secretaries and drivers left their tasks to come to the editor's office.

Employee: Congratulations to the new director!

Employee: Good luck to our leader!

Ramos (runs in excitedly, goes over to Domínguez and embraces him): You have saved *The Tribune* from total collapse! I had faith in you. I knew very well that you wouldn't refuse.

Domínguez (surrounded by the group): This outpouring of loyalty fills me with happiness. I must tell you I never believed I had so many supporters. This is a revelation to me. If I had known it before, I wouldn't have thought twice before accepting the job!

Ramos (shouting): Long live Domínguez!

All (in chorus): Long may he live!

Domínguez: Thank you. I'm very touched. Please don't continue or I'll start to cry.

Ramos: Don't worry, boss, we promise unconditional cooperation. Isn't that right, people?

All: Yes, we promise!

Domínguez: Well, that's enough, and I thank you with all my heart. Now let's work in a united and organized way. My intention is that *The Tribune* continue as a responsible paper given the crisis of the moment. That is our first duty to ourselves and, above all, to our readers...

Moncada: That's the way to talk!

Domínguez (walking back and forth): First of all, we will dedicate the front page of tomorrow's edition to our assassinated colleagues. Have their bodies, or as much as they've found of them, brought here. We will make them a posthumous offering in the halls on the first floor. We will invite our respected friend, Monsignor Romero, to officiate at the funeral. And all of this will be published in *The Tribune*, because the heroism of our deceased brothers in the profession must be remembered with great respect.

Moncada (shouting): Now you're talking! That's what we'll do!

Domínguez: The funeral will be a very proper ceremony!

Moncada: Yes, we'll install powerful loudspeakers around the building, so that everyone can hear Monsignor Romero's voice...

Ramos: We'll invite the popular organizations to make an appearance so that their signs and banners can denounce the brutal assassination of the reporter and the photographer.

Domínguez: Let's proceed!

THE REVOLUTIONARY COORDINATOR OF THE MASSES CALLS A GENERAL STRIKE. MILITARY OPERATIONS IN HACIENDA COLIMA, SUCHITOTO, PLAN DE OCOTES, EL ROSARIO, LA LAGUNA, ARCATAO, NATIONAL UNIVERSITY, SANTA TECLA, LEAVE MORE THAN 150 VICTIMS. EMPLOYEE OF *THE INDEPENDENT* NEWSPAPER MACHINE-GUNNED TO DEATH.

Lately, due to the shortage of employees and the growing popularity of *The Tribune*, we had been working overtime almost every day. Tonight, when I left work, I had only enough energy to stop to have supper in a restaurant and go directly to the boarding house. As usual, I would visit Lourdes. Perhaps I would be lucky enough to find her still awake so that we could talk for a while.

I entered the boarding house through the main door. The lights were on and the accountant, the mechanic and his wife, who held the baby in her arms, were out in the middle of the courtyard. Simón, his wife and children were there, too.

"Rogelio!" exclaimed the accountant. "Where were you?!"

"What do you mean where was I? Working. Why?"

"I thought you had been arrested," said Simón, surprised.

"What are you all talking about? What's going on?"

"A little while ago some men came to search the boarding house. They didn't say whom or what they were looking for. They turned over furniture and threw everything on the floor."

As Simón was talking to me, I began to walk toward my room and they all followed me.

"They destroyed my paintings!" was my first reaction. My room was a complete disaster: torn paintings; paint spilled all over the floor; chairs and tables smashed; pieces of the mattress strewn throughout the room; the bed overturned.

"Miss Lourdes' room is the same," lamented Simón's wife.

"And where is she!" I screamed, seized by a horrible fear, rushing out toward Lourdes' room, and finding it, too, in disorder when I entered. "Where is she!" I shouted again, but no one knew how to answer my desperate questions.

"I think she's just not home yet," said the accountant finally. "I know that she's usually home by now. But who knows why she's late today?"

"They've left the house in ruins," Simón said bitterly, comforting one of his children who could not stop crying. "They terrorized us! The poor children were screaming in fear because of the threats. They're so frightened they can't sleep."

"At least they didn't hurt anyone," said the mechanic's wife. "In these situations, the best thing is just to be quiet and let them do as they wish."

Simón's wife was drying her tears in silence. The children were still crying, clinging to their mother's skirts. Their little faces showed the traces of an early fear that already assailed their innocence. Their little eyes looked around in confusion.

"Mami, mami, I'm afraid, hold me."

I was trying to think where I could find Lourdes, but I couldn't think of any place she might be. So I began to pick up my room, hoping she would arrive soon. About midnight I heard the main door open and we all went out to see who it was. It was Simoncito returning from the university. We were very happy to see him safe and sound. I returned to my room. As I waited anxiously, the dawn arrived, but Lourdes did not.

Monsignor Romero: In rural areas, according to the Amnesty spokesman, at least 3,500 peasants are presently fleeing from their homes toward the capital, trying to save themselves from the persecution. "We have complete lists in London and Sweden of children, youth, and women who have been assassinated because they were organized," declared Fuentes. The informant said that Amnesty International, which is a humanitarian organization, does not identify with governments, organizations, or individuals; "we are not attempting to overthrow the government but we are fighting for human rights to be respected in every part of the world...especially where they are most threatened or trampled on," said Fuentes. This confirms, therefore, what we are reporting about this frightening week.

I would like to analyze, with regard to this very violent day of the 17th, what was perhaps the cause of that violence, the strike called by the Revolutionary Coordinator of the Masses.

Its purpose was a protest against the repression, and last Sunday I said that the purpose is a legitimate one. It is an attempt to denounce a situation that is intolerable. But the strike also had a political intention, to demonstrate that the repression, rather than intimidating the popular organizations, was fortifying them, and to reject the opposition of the current government which needs violent repression to carry out its reforms. Reforms which for many reasons are not acceptable to the popular organizations.

The martial law and misinformation to which we have been subjected, and the official communiqués as well as the majority of our communications media, do not as yet permit objective measurement of the extent of the national strike. Foreign radio stations have spoken of 70% effectiveness, which would certainly be an extremely high proportion, and could be regarded as a notable triumph. Even without counting the establishments that closed out of fear of actions by the left as well as those carried out by the right and the government early that same Monday morning, it cannot be denied that the strength shown by the Coordinator, strictly in the field of labor, was great. The Coordinator is strong not only in the country but also in the factories and the city.

It is very probable that errors were committed. But in spite of all those mistakes, one can see that the strike was an advance in the popular struggle and was a demonstration of the fact that the left can paralyze the economic activity of the country... The response of the government to the strike was certainly harsh. Not only do the patrolling of the city and the shooting at the University of El Salvador demonstrate this, but above all, the deaths that they caused. No less than 10 workers were killed by the security forces in the factories on strike; even three workers from the Mayor's Office were found murdered after having been detained by agents of the Treasury Police. And this is a clear denunciation from the Mayor's Office in the capital itself...

But in addition to these deaths there were others the same day, up to a minimum of 60 according to some, and others say there were more than 140. And the labor stoppage was accompanied in the countryside by combative activities by some of the popular organizations. Such was the case in Colima, San Martín, and Suchitoto. Although the tactical advisability of these operations by the organizations may be doubted, this possible impropriety did not justify the repressive action of the government.

Certainly the Coordinator has shortcomings and has a long way to go to become a coherent alternative of democratic revolutionary power. It is to be hoped that they will evaluate and work on perfecting an expression that is truly of the people and that they will not, in their blunders, encounter the repudiation of the people themselves. They are a hope, a solution, if they mature and become truly understanding of the desires of the people.

Their shortcomings, nevertheless, are not the result of their being subversives, or hoodlums, or delinquents, which they are not; those shortcomings are the result of not being permitted a normal political development. They are persecuted, massacred, impeded in their efforts to organize, in their attempts to extend their relations with other democratic groups. This will only lead to their radicalization and desperation. It is unlikely under these circumstances that they will not resort to revolutionary activities, to combative struggles. The least that can be said is that the country is experiencing a pre-revolutionary stage and by no means a stage of transition.

The next morning, extremely worried by Lourdes' absence, I went to wait for the bus on my way to work. The night had been one of terrible uncertainty, anxiety, and sleeplessness.

Across the street, several people were examining some dead bodies they had discovered in the garbage, trying to establish their identity. My curiosity made me cross the street. The people covered their noses as they used broom handles to frighten away the rats that were hidden among the decomposing bodies. I felt a great relief upon ascertaining that none of the dead looked anything like Lourdes. I returned to join the group that was waiting for the bus. The incident across the street continued to be the topic of conversation among several people. Others were talking about how expensive everything was and how easy it was to be found dead in the middle of the street in the morning.

A dilapidated bus stopped and we got on. Although it was already full, interestingly, we all fit.

In the crowded bus, I thought about Lourdes and about how much my life had changed in the last five months. Survival had become less complicated even in the midst of the violence and terrorism. I had a job and had paid all my debts. My ulcers had disappeared and I was able to give myself the luxury of eating at least twice a day. I had a friend and protector, Domínguez, who had opened my eyes to life and to the harsh reality of our country. My job at *The Tribune* had accelerated that understanding. Lourdes, my first true love, had opened my heart to the land, to poetry, and to the popular causes. In all, the last five months had been one of the most important chapters in my life. And it had all happened so fast.

Next to me, to my right, stood a man in a white shirt and dark glasses, carrying a handful of books. The bus arrived at my destination. As I squeezed through the crowd toward the door, I felt someone reach into my pants' pocket. I looked back, and the man in the dark glasses smiled amiably. Once out on the street, I checked my pockets and was relieved to find my wallet, but surprised to find a note. I recognized Lourdes' handwriting immediately. "I'll meet you at the Central Market, 1:00 p.m. Entrance opposite El Calvario."

That was the longest morning of my life. Finally at 12:30, and I rushed out of the office toward the market.

The noontime heat was intense as always. The area around the market was crowded with vendors who, in addition to hawking their wares, were being careful to avoid being surprised by the Municipal Police or run over by trucks, cars, and busses.

Inside the market, interminable criss-crossing hallways, dark and narrow, were lined with small stores filled with merchandise, odors, voices, colors, music, and shouts. I walked among the men, women, and children who carried baskets, bags, and sacks, moving actively in all directions. The mixture of constant and varied noises formed a deafening hum. I was invaded by a strange sensation, as though I were inside a huge beehive.

I stopped to get something to drink at El Rinconcito, a tiny business squeezed in between a shoe store and a clothing shop. I was waited on by a woman who was busy washing large jugs in a big aluminum pot as she sang along, in a shrill, off-key voice, with the song on the radio. On the dark walls of the little shop hung calendars with foreign landscapes surrounding a faded reproduction of Saint Jude, framed beneath broken and smokey glass, covered with cobwebs. Next to the saint hung a black scapulary, like an insect with very long antennae.

"What can I give you?" asked the woman with the shrill voice, snapping me out of my observations. "I have horchata, tamarindo, ensalada, granadilla, cebada..."

"Horchata, please."

The woman took a large ladle and deftly stirred the drink as she sang along with Camilo Sesto.

"May I never be without you, never, never, nor without the warmth of your way of loving, never..."

"That song really gets to me," she said with a smile that revealed her dark, broken teeth. "Horchata you said?"

"Yes, please."

"Here it is; it's nice and cold," she assured me, handing me the cup that was almost overflowing.

I was savoring the horchata and examining my surroundings when, suddenly, I saw that the man with the white shirt and dark glasses was approaching. With a light movement of his head and a friendly smile, he indicated that I should follow him. I left the cup on the counter and once again joined the tumult of packages and people in the corridors. Someone touched my shoulder and said "hi." I turned my gaze toward the voice and my eyes met the face of a woman with short brown hair and dark glasses so big that they almost covered her entire face.

"Hi, it's me."

"Oh, hi; Lourdes?"

"Yes, it's me; don't you remember me anymore? Gosh, you sure forgot me in a hurry."

"I didn't recognize you," I said, taking her hand, restraining my impulse to hug and kiss her. "You look so different. Really, unrecognizable."

"I'm wearing a wig," she said, putting her delicate arms around my waist, walking next to me as if we were walking through Venustiano Carranza Park as we had so many times.

"I've been worried sick about you since last night when I got home and found they had searched the place and you didn't come back."

"They were looking for me," she said without emotion. "Several of us have been fingered. Three teachers have already disappeared. There are spies among us. My contacts warned me. If they catch me, I'm dead. So I've been forced to go underground. It's very possible that this is the last time we'll ever see each other."

"Now I understand the intensity with which you used to talk to me," I said, caressing her silky neck.

The man in the white shirt walked past in front of us.

"I have to go," said Lourdes calmly, opening one of my hands with her soft fingers and depositing there a roll of papers. "These are my latest poems."

"When can I see you?" I whispered, suddenly holding her back and embracing her tenderly, wishing that that moment would last forever.

"I don't know," she said, without changing her passive, cool expression. "Really, I don't know."

"Wait," I said, afraid of losing her. "Wait, don't go yet."

I took her face in my hands and delicately kissed her sweaty forehead.

"The people will overcome!" she said, and the words came out like a muted shout that got caught in her throat.

Lourdes walked away behind the man in the white shirt and both disappeared in the labyrinth of hallways overflowing with people.

Outside the market, the heat had not diminished. Now I walked along murmuring the name that completely occupied my mind. Lourdes. Happy and delicate, determined and rebellious. Smile, beauty, intelligence and courage combined in one person. Lourdes. With whom I had shared joys, sorrows, and unforgettable adventures; the marvelous being who had opened her generous crystalline world to me. A young woman dedicated heart and soul to humanity, who preached to me the word of solidarity with the people during long nights of wakefulness, visions, love, art, poetry. Who loved me with so much strength and fervor, as if focusing her love for all humanity on me.

Now I ask myself if I deserved the tender gaze of her big, beautiful black eyes, the freshness of her open, childlike smile. Possibly my own independence, or selfishness, never permitted me to love her with all the humanism and intensity with which she loved me.

I stopped at the corner and opened one of the moist papers which still smelled of her perfume.

> Our love
> is the envy of space
> and time.
> Reality erects strong walls
> of pain and blood
> to isolate and dissolve
> this love I have for you.
> But this deep and burning love
> will not die,
> for it is now a humble offering
> to our suffering people.
>
> Lourdes.

Monsignor Romero: The fundamental question is how to get out of this critical period by the least violent path. And in this regard, the greatest responsibility lies with the civilian and, above all, the military authorities. I hope they will not allow themselves to be blinded by what they are doing in the area of agrarian reform. It may be an illusion that keeps them from seeing the totality of the problem.

On Tuesday—we are following a week filled with events that cannot go without mention. In the newspaper clippings that I brought about the Pope, the Holy Father too points out the number of victims there have been in Italy and Rome, especially during those days. This means, therefore, that if the Pope were in my place, he would mention not only the 10 cruel assassinations in Italy but would take the time, as we do here, to keep track day by day of the many, many assassinations.

On March 18 the bodies of four peasants were found, in different areas, two in Metapán, two in San Miguel.

On Wednesday, March 19, at 5:30 in the morning, after a military operation in the cantons of San Luis La Loma, La Cayetana, León de Piedra, La India, Paz, Opico, and El Mono, the bodies of three peasants were found: Humberto Urbino, Oswaldo Hernández, and Francisco García.

In the capital, at two o'clock in the afternoon, the offices of the Beverages Unions and the Revolutionary Union Federation were occupied militarily while many workers were holding a wake over the body of Manuel Pacín, a worker who was also an advisor to the municipal workers, whose body was found in Apulo, after he was captured. In this occupation, two persons were killed, including worker Mauricio Barrera, director of the Mechanical and Metallic Industries Union.

Nineteen workers were turned over to the courts. At the request of their relatives, Legal Aid is intervening in this case. It has been reported that the files of the unions were confiscated.

In the national press, there was a report of the deaths of nine peasants in a battle, according to the Armed Forces, in the town of San Bartolo Tecoluca. At noon, Army soldiers in the town of El Almendral, jurisdiction of Majagual, La Libertad, captured peasants Miguel Angel Gómez de Paz, Concepción Coralia Menjívar, and José Emilio Valencia, and they have not yet been freed. We ask that they be turned over to the courts.

On Thursday, March 20, at four o'clock in the afternoon, in Cantón El Jocote, Quetzaltepeque, peasant leader Alfonso Muñoz Pacheco, Secretary of Conflicts of the Federation of Field Workers, was assassinated. Mr. Muñoz was widely known in the country for his dedication to the cause of the peasants.

And something very horrible, very important, on this same day, Thursday the 20th—peasant Agustín Sánchez was found still alive. He had been captured on the 15th in Zacatecoluca by soldiers who turned him over to the Treasury Police. Mr. Sánchez has declared, in a statement before a notary and witnesses, that his capture occurred in Hacienda El Cauca, Department of La Paz, when he was working on membership for the Salvadoran Communal Union. For four days they tortured him, without food or water, with constant beatings and suffocation, until March 19th when, together with two other companions, he was shot in the head, but luckily in his case this bullet only destroyed his right cheek and eye. Near death in the early morning, some peasants helped him until a trusted person could take him to the capital. This horrendous testimonial could not be signed by the peasant, because his hands were destroyed. Persons of unquestioned good name witnessed this horrible scene and there are photographs that reveal the condition in which this poor peasant was found.

We also have a report, still unconfirmed, of the mass killing of 25 peasants, in San Pablo Tacachico. At the last minute, at the start of our Mass, the confirmation of this terrible tragedy arrived. It says that on Friday the 21st of this month, starting at six o'clock in the morning, a military operation was carried out along the road from Santa Ana to San Pablo Tacachico. Said operation was carried out by soldiers from the headquarters of Opico and Santa Ana together with the Treasury Police, stationed in Tacachico, who had with them a list of suspects. In this operation searches were conducted in the cantons of El Resbaladero, San Felipe, Moncagua, El Portillo, San José La Cova, Mogotes and their respective neighborhoods, Los Pozos and Las Delicias. During the operation they also searched everyone who was riding on busses or walking.

In Cantón Mogotes, jurisdiction of Tacachico, the repression was more cruel, for troops with two tanks terrorized the inhabitants of this sector. In the search they carried out, they stole four radios and 400 colones in cash, and they burned the home and all the belongings of Rosalio Cruz who, together with his family, finds himself in the worst poverty. They assassinated Alejandro Mojica and Félix Santos, the first in his home and the second in a ravine. Both leave widows and orphaned children. Out of fear of repression, both men were buried in their own yards. In addition, Isabel Cruz, Manuel Santos, and Santos Urquilla were taken away, their destination unknown.

One final report, with which we wish to express a special solidarity. Yesterday afternoon the UCA, Central American University, was attacked for the first time and without provocation. A powerful, bellicose team undertook this operation at

1:15 in the afternoon with the National Police. They entered the campus shooting, and a student who was studying math, Manuel Orantes Guillén, was assassinated. I am also told that several students have disappeared and that their relatives and the UCA are protesting the invasion of a campus which should be respected in its autonomy. What they have not done at the National University, undoubtedly because of fear, they have done at the UCA, and the UCA has shown that it is not armed to defend itself and that it has been trampled upon without any motive. We hope to give more details of this serious breach against civilization and legality in our country.

Dear brethren, it would be interesting now to analyze what these months of a new government which intended to bring us out of these horrible times has meant, but I do not wish to abuse of your time. And if what they are trying to do is to decapitate the organization of the people and impede the process that the people want, no other process can go forward. Without its roots in the people, no government can be effective, much less when it wants to implant them by force through blood and pain.

I would like to make a special appeal to the men of the Army and specifically to the bases of the National Guard, the Police, and the military.

Brothers, you are our own people; you are killing your own peasant brothers and sisters; and against an order to kill given by a man, the law of God, which says DO NOT KILL, must prevail. No soldier is compelled to obey an order contrary to the law of God. No one need comply with an immoral law. It is time for you to regain your conscience and obey your conscience and not the order of sin. The church, defender of God-given rights, of God's law, of human and personal dignity, cannot remain silent in the face of such abomination. We want the government to take seriously that reforms which come stained with so much blood are worthless. In the name of God, therefore, and in the name of this suffering people whose cries rise to the heavens more tumultuously each day, I beg you, I implore you, I order you in the name of God: Stop the repression!...

MONSIGNOR ROMERO IS ASSASSINATED.

Editor's office. The photographer pushes the office door open and begins to shout desperately.

Ramos: They killed Monsignor Romero! They killed Monsignor Romero!

(Several employees hear the shouts of the photographer and come running in, incredulous, asking all kinds of questions. Ramos continues shouting and running from office to office. The phone rings insistently. Domínguez appears not to believe the shouts. He answers the phone. He listens with great attention. After a few minutes he throws down the phone and sinks into his chair. He remains still, head down, without moving even a muscle of the exhausted body that seems to have been abandoned on the chair in a dark corner. Rogelio seems hypnotized, staring toward the window: Moncada enters the office, upset like everyone else, but making an effort to keep his composure. Other employees come and go, refusing to believe the news that now comes not only from the photographer's mouth, but the authenticity of which has been confirmed by the telephone calls which are still coming in to the newspaper.)

Moncada (approaching Domínguez): I suggest that, as director, you should write something...

(The administrator cannot contain his emotion either. His voice breaks. His eyes become wet. He takes a few indecisive steps and leaves the office. The editorial room is silent. Moncada returns a few moments later.)

Moncada: Well, Domínguez...

(The director has not moved; he is still sitting with his eyes fixed on the dirty floor of the office.)

Moncada: A posthumous offering...

Domínguez (without raising his eyes): Look Moncada, leave me alone; you and *The Tribune* itself can go to hell... Even if I write the best article of my life, it won't fix anything... It's too late... Everything is lost... This is hell...

Moncada (addressing Rogelio): I understand those feelings very well. Most Salvadorans feel the same way.

Rogelio (recovering his composure somewhat): It's an abominable thing.

Moncada: You, Villaverde, as the director's assistant, are the one to do it. You have sufficient experience.

Rogelio: Not enough to write editorials, much less in such a serious case, one of such great importance.

Moncada: I know very well you have the ability to do it.

Rogelio: Since you insist, I will do the best I can.

Moncada: Very well, I'll be sending you the necessary information. We have an extensive file on the life and work of Monsignor. Write it today and we will publish it tomorrow.

(Moncada leaves and Rogelio begins to look through papers in search of recent reports.)

Rogelio (talking out loud to himself): I doubt that I can write an editorial appropriate to the importance of this case...

Domínguez (finally coming out of his stupor): Go home, Rogelio, don't worry. I'll write it, even if I have to stay up all night. Go home; it's late.

Rogelio (before leaving approaches Domínguez and tenderly puts an arm around his shoulders): See you tomorrow.

(He leaves and closes the door. Domínguez again remains motionless in his chair, holding his head in his hands, his elbows on the desk, as if studying the strange shapes made by the ink as his tears fall on the paper.)

I was overcome by a feeling of being cold inside, a chilling of my soul, that made me feel strangely alone, weak, abandoned.

At the bus stop, frightful comments of destruction and death could be heard. Suddenly the city became dark. A storm was approaching. Gigantic dark clouds swirled in the sky as if they were going to crash down on San Salvador. Intermittent flashes of lightning split the gray sky like fissures of silver. The wind formed whirlwinds which in rapid spirals blew garbage through the street, smashing it into walls that were stained with sinister blood-colored slogans. For a moment the city was gripped by a lethal silence, a suspense perhaps like that which invaded the earth moments before the Universal Flood.

As the bus arrived, strong explosions were heard in the area. The passengers, in the blink of an eye, got out of the vehicle and began to run toward stores and warehouses in search of refuge. New explosions shook the area. People screamed that the civil war had finally broken out. Children cried, their faces buried in the skirts of their mothers who clung to their purses, bags, and baskets.

"It's the end of the world!" exclaimed a woman as she crossed herself. "God will not permit the assassination of Monsignor Romero to go unpunished!"

An elderly woman prayed the Ave María aloud, kneeling to kiss the filthy floor of the pharmacy where we had taken refuge. Several young men tried in vain to calm the women who were crying and, in their desperation, were abandoning baskets of fruit in the middle of the street. The explosions and shooting seemed to be coming from the same block where the pharmacy that protected us was located.

"The guerrillas are taking the city!" shouted the owner of the business. He asked us to help him close the doors and windows; then he turned out the lights.

We threw ourselves to the floor and kept silent. Some whispered prayers. Others moaned and sighed.

Face down on the muddy floor I thought about Lourdes, about Domínguez, about Ignacio, about Monsignor Romero, about El Salvador, about all of us who were lying there on the floor. We all appeared to share the same dark fate.

A half-hour later the explosions ceased. The owner opened one window a crack, then another and lastly the door. Out in the street, the situation seemed to have returned to normal. The storm dissipated. The driver ran to the bus and we all followed him. In a couple of minutes we had all boarded the bus, which took off at great speed, disobeying the stoplights and not stopping at the bus stops.

An elderly woman lost consciousness and collapsed on the floor. We picked her up and put her on a seat which a woman carrying a basket of sweet rolls kindly gave up. We fanned her with newspapers, but the scant air barely circulated among the huge crowd of passengers. The woman did not regain consciousness.

The bus was going through Barrio San Jacinto. I decided to get out near the Capitol Movie Theater and stop at Ignacio's brother's house.

"Hi, Rogelio," he said, surprised. "I haven't seen you for a long time. Come in quick and let's close the door before we get hit by a stray bullet."

We had supper with the radio turned way up to hear the latest news about the death of Monsignor Romero. It was discouraging to hear that, by decree of the Government Junta, the stations were prohibited from reporting about the assassination. Instead they played popular music and the usual commercials.

"As if the dark situation we're in were insignificant," commented Ignacio's brother, "and the stench of death in the city were an unimportant incident.

"Their purpose is to keep us completely isolated from reality. One of these mornings someone will wake up and go outside and find that he is the only survivor, in a ghost city full of ashes, skeletons and vultures."

In the distance the echoes of gunshots and explosions could be heard. We finished eating and I went into Ignacio's studio.

The painting "The Enemy of the People" was in the center of the room, surrounded by other no less violent compositions. I decided to look through things, find an empty canvas, brushes and paint. I felt, more than inspiration, an urgency to paint, to form with shape and color the confused ideas whirling in my brain.

I put the empty canvas on a frame. I looked for an easel. I put the colors out on a piece of wood. The brushes moved between my nervous fingers. I began to splash them on the canvas, uncertain of what I would paint.

Hours later the canvas showed a figure dressed in white with his hands placed on the heads of ragged children, afflicted women, wounded men. The multitude crowded around the white figure who remained standing, untiring, imparting, with his benevolent smile, a message of peace and hope. I planned to title the painting "The Guardian of Hope."

It was early morning now and I felt completely exhausted. I put the brushes aside, turned out the light, and lay down on a sofa. The images of the crowd surrounding Monsignor Romero gradually faded. The benevolent smile of the priest became the soft pillow of my dreams.

The next morning I was awakened by Ignacio's brother knocking on the door, telling me that breakfast was ready.

I jumped up. Monsignor's smile, still stuck in my mind, reminded me of last night's painting. I turned on the light so I could admire it.

There was the painting. Buildings, houses, and destroyed shacks. Mountains of dead bodies surrounded a man in a white robe, who was also lying in the street, next to a golden crucifix, his broken body dripping blood. I didn't remember having painted this scene. Surely the other, the one I had planned to call "The Guardian of Hope," had been just a dream.

"What a sad painting," said Ignacio's brother. "I wonder who killed Monsignor: the assassin's bullet, or his own courage in defending the oppressed."

"No one can take the life of one who has already surrendered it to his neighbor," I said, leaving the studio. "Because that surrender is born out of love for humanity. And that love never dies."

EDITORIAL

Monsignor Oscar Arnulfo Romero y Galdámez was assassinated by a gunshot on Monday, March 24, 1980 at 6:30 in the afternoon, while officiating at a funeral mass in Divine Providence Chapel in the capital.

According to statements taken in the emergency room of the Salvadoran Polyclinic where the archbishop was taken, a shot rang out at the precise moment when Monsignor Romero was finishing his homily and preparing for the consecration of the bread and wine. The priest collapsed at the foot of a crucifix. When more shots were heard in the street, those present at the religious service tried to save themselves. They testify to having seen four men flee and another escape in a red Volkswagen car.

In the emergency room and halls of the Polyclinic there was a huge crowd of priests, religious and lay people, and relatives trying to see the Archbishop, whose body lay lifeless, still in its priestly vestments, a small bullet hole right next to his heart.

It was noted that this is the first case in Central America in which a high dignitary of the Catholic Church has been assassinated during a religious ceremony.

Monsignor Romero was born in Ciudad Barrios, in the Department of San Miguel, at 3:00 a.m. on August 15, 1917.

His parents were Santos Romero and Guadalupe de Jesús Galdámez. He did his pastoral studies at Pío Latinoamericano College of Rome, the city where on April 2, 1942 he was ordained. For several years he was Secretary of the Chamber of Ecclesiastical Government of the San Miguel Diocese. Serving San Francisco and El Rosario churches, he became Rector of the Metropolitan Cathedral, later serving in Santiago de María as Bishop of that city. He was elected Archbishop of San Salvador on February 20, 1977.

The exercise of his duties as Archbishop was difficult even from the beginning. Less than one month after having taken the position, he had to confront with courage the sad and violent death of a cleric—Father Rutilio Grande, who was assassinated March 12, 1977 in the takeover of Aguilares; a child and an elderly man who were with him also perished. Within a three-year period the number of assassinated clergy grew to seven. Monsignor Romero's name is now added to the somber list.

Faced with the events and demands of his time, Monsignor Romero became the voice of the oppressed, social, political, and Christian all in one, and a revolutionary symbol, since he advocated profound social changes.

His constant and determined words in defense of human rights were recognized internationally. In Europe he was awarded three peace prizes. The University of Louvain in Belgium and Georgetown University in the United States nominated him Doctor "Honoris Causa." In 1979, Monsignor Romero was nominated for the Nobel Peace Prize by members of the British Parliament and the United States Congress.

Many sectors of Salvadoran society had faith that the pastoral light of Monsignor Romero would illuminate the best alternative, a peaceful and coherent one, that would provide the solution to the socio-political crisis of our country. His untiring voice denounced the errors and violence of the military and oligarchical fronts, showing them that they had the obligation to seek a process of change based on peaceful cooperation and understanding. Faced with the negligence of the ruling regime in establishing realistic reforms to benefit the poor classes, he finally recognized the legitimate right of the people to organize themselves and, if necessary, to resort to a revolutionary struggle to free themselves from repression.

The body of the Archbishop was taken to the National Basilica, where it will lie in state. The Metropolitan Curia has declared three days of National Mourning, which will also be observed by all the Catholic schools.

The Government Junta also decreed three days of National Mourning. The members of the Junta said they hoped that the death of the prelate would not cause more violence in our country, since Monsignor Romero advocated the reign of peace among all the people of El Salvador.

The Tribune, upon reporting this diabolical deed that has moved all Salvadorans, condemns this most vile assassination and has faith that the investigations in the case will reveal the motives and perpetrators of the crime. Monsignor Romero, the principal Pastor of the Salvadoran Catholic faith, died in the exercise of his Christian mission, and his assassination is an outrage against the most sacred principles of humanity. It puts the moral values of our society in doubt. It is a sacrilege that forces us to conclude that our people have been denied, in a demagogical way, the most minimal advancement in human development. They have been forced to regress to the most primitive state of the species.

Anyone who resorts to attacking the spiritual representatives of our society by violent means and sacrilegious acts demonstrates no other intention than that of institutionalizing a cruel and bloody control that will destroy every vestige of hope for the decent existence of our citizenry.

Remember, all who may have participated in perpetrating this abominable act, whoever you may be, that your plans can never materialize. NEVER. Because this suffering people will not permit it. Because there still exist brave men willing to continue the struggle on behalf of the cause of the oppressed.

Because if the assassins achieve their goals, it would mean total destruction, the death of men of good will, the end of democratic hope in the world.

But, no matter how much those who advocate violence terrorize, our world is not lost, nor is it on the brink of destruction, although it may seem to be, because our humanity hides and jealously preserves an invaluable essence of love and hope that will save it from total chaos. Because behind each despot a Monsignor Romero marches bravely. Because not even the most cruel assassin will destroy the sweetness of the world. Because these beasts of terror succumb to their own poison. And the world continues its marked rotation in the humanism that sustains it. That is our hope. The sacred hope of humanity.

Monsignor Romero has been assassinated. Incredible but true. But let it be known clearly and perfectly well that his word has not died. His voice remains forever etched on the hearts of Salvadorans, and will echo eternally in our land of crosses, tears, and blood of innocent children.

They have killed the man but not his spirit, because the light of his ideals is infinite. Because even from the tomb he will speak to us untiringly of God, of struggle, of hope, of love.

The Tribune

MONSIGNOR ROMERO'S BODY IS TRANSFERRED
TO THE CATHEDRAL IN A PROCESSION OF 5,000
PEOPLE. FUNERAL SERVICES ARE ANNOUNCED FOR
PALM SUNDAY.

That morning everyone got up early. Simón and his family were the first to use the bathroom and the kitchen. They were in a hurry to leave for the Cathedral to get a good place in Gerardo Barrios Plaza from which to witness the funeral of Monsignor Romero.

"Hurry up, Simón," pressured his wife. "We have to leave as soon as possible because we have to walk downtown. The busses aren't running today."

"Rogelio, do you want to come with us?" they asked before they left.

"Thanks, Don Simón, but I'm not ready yet. Maybe I'll see you there."

The whole family left the house wearing their Sunday best. The children were bathed, their hair combed and shining. She, dressed in mourning. Simón wearing the black shoes he had been polishing since he learned of the death of Monsignor Romero. Bolaños and his wife, carrying the baby in her arms, followed by the accountant and other tenants, were also getting ready to leave.

"Rogelio," Bolaños called to me before leaving, "let's see about having a few drinks after the funeral."

"Be quiet," his wife interrupted. "All you think about is drinking."

"It's not just to drink," he argued. "It's also in memory of Monsignor. Right, Rogelio?"

"We'll talk about it when we get back," I said, accompanying them to the door. "See you later."

On the way back to my room I passed the one Lourdes used to occupy and, without thinking, I knocked on the door. Seconds later, when no one responded, I came to and remembered her absence.

All was silent in the boarding house, tranquil solitude. I walked down the hall past the rooms, and fragments of the past began to file through my mind. Not completely happy times, but times when Lourdes' voice eclipsed the spaces of unhappiness. Now it had all been hushed. All I had left of her were her poems. Her voice and her smile existed only in my memory.

I reentered my room struggling with the memories. They took over, forcing me to seek out the handful of poems Lourdes gave me the last time I saw her. Reading them, I felt that her voice calmed my anxiety.

That morning, inexplicably, it was very difficult for me to start the day. I couldn't find the white shirt that I had set aside for this very important occasion. I wandered about the room with a certain drowsiness. It must have been 9:30 when I finally left the boarding house.

Out in the street, people were walking in small groups, hurrying to reach the Cathedral before the funeral began. The morning was sunny, the sky wearing its best blue shirt. The sky seemed to predict a magnificent day. Nevertheless, that very fact caused me certain distrust. Perhaps because the week that was ending passed with greater turbulence than usual. And it's not that violence wasn't customary here; we Salvadorans all know that; we feel it in our own flesh and bones, to the point that one wonders what things would be like without the daily terrorism we've all grown used to, how people in other parts of the world feel, people who don't have to be awakened at midnight by shootings and bombings, wondering who has died this time. A relative? An acquaintance? A guerrilla? A Guardsman? With the fear that the door will be kicked in and we'll be taken out into the street naked by aggressors who ignore, without compassion, the pleas of mothers, children and wives. One wonders if in other countries people have to be faced every morning with nauseating scenes of tortured bodies abandoned on the sidewalks, with no alternative other than to close their eyes and cover their noses as they continue on their way to work. Many times we do not even question these things because they have become an essential part of our reality. Part of our folklore. So natural that it is difficult for us to be shocked at them. We have lost the ability to be surprised, to be frightened by death. Perhaps out of fear that our neighbor may hear our complaints and resentment, that he may read our minds and finger us, label us subversives for complaining about the pervasive stench of death, and that we ourselves will then be the ones who are found covered with flies the next day, ours the bodies discovered by the stray dogs who, like the vultures, are now fed by the abundance of human flesh.

I was walking through Barrio La Vega thinking that the death of Monsignor Romero had left a deep wound in the hearts of the people, a mixed sensation of desolation, impotence and indignation. We all pictured the assassin differently, and each of us punished him according to our own capacity to hate, according to the intensity of our repudiation of such a horrendous act of violence.

People hurried to the funeral, expressions of rage and insolence on their haggard, drawn faces. Some dared to shout insults against the government. They were not afraid to make their hatred public. In their faces the thirst for vengeance burned, but their fallen arms showed resignation and their uncertain steps reflected impotence. That was the chronicle of the week.

Some of those walking were commenting about the suspicious absence of the security forces.

"They're cowards. They're afraid. They know that if we find them out on the street we'll give it to them. We'll eat them alive."

Others alleged just the opposite.

"Of course they're watching us. But they're dressed in civilian clothes so they won't be recognized."

In this way we arrived at the steep street that the National Police Headquarters is on. No one dared to walk on that side. We all crossed the street to the sidewalk in front of San Alfonso Marista School.

A couple of days ago Domínguez had asked me to go with him to the funeral. Through his connections he had gotten permission to attend the ceremony inside the Cathedral. But I preferred to watch it from outside. At this moment my boss was very near the remains of his friend.

During the previous week, *The Tribune* had dedicated several pages to the life and work of Monsignor Romero, and had reported on the funeral plans. The popular organizations had invited the people to meet this Sunday in Cuscatlán Park and march from there to the Cathedral. Another procession of priests and novices of different religious orders would leave from the Basilica. The Government Junta, on the other hand, had promised to keep the security forces in their headquarters, removed from the ceremony, in order to avoid confrontations.

Everything seemed to indicate that the country had called a truce to bury Monsignor Romero in a solemn and peaceful ceremony. According to the announcements, ecclesiastical authorities from all parts of the world would be present at the funeral. A rumor was even circulating that the Pope himself would be present. Officially, Cardinal Ernesto Corripio Ahumada of Mexico would represent the main religious authority as the personal envoy of John Paul II.

I was remembering these details as I was walking near Gerardo Barrios Plaza, in the very center of San Salvador. Now people were forced to walk slowly because as we got closer to the plaza it became more difficult to move. It was as if the five million inhabitants of El Salvador were all gathered in the center of the city.

It must have been about 10:30 in the morning when I walked past the eastern side of the National Palace, which was also located on the plaza. My idea was to position myself near the main entrance to the Cathedral, but it was almost impossible to walk through the dense crowd. With great effort, half an hour later I managed to reach one of the corners of the plaza located in front of the church, and could advance no farther. I had to be content with watching the ceremony from there, able only to make out a jumbled group of clergy congregated at the entrance to the temple.

Earth
Something tells me that you still exist.
That the grandeur of the Mayas
is hidden
in the eyes of some child.

Earth
Defend this divine and ancestral
treasure of your structure.

Because
The soul of our ancient gods
has been unleashed
in your furrow.

Because
The blood which has been shed
begins to build
the new day.

Lourdes

All the approaches to the massive, unfinished monument that was the Cathedral had been closed to contain the multitude of the faithful in Gerardo Barrios Plaza and its surroundings. The inside of the temple was reserved for special guests, relatives and close friends of Monsignor Romero, and national and foreign ecclesiastical authorities.

This day, Palm Sunday, March 30, 1980, the entire country, and perhaps most of the world, had its eyes on the funeral of the man they now called "the martyr of the dispossessed."

Beneath the arch of the main entrance a wooden altar had been constructed, where about 300 clerics celebrated Mass together with Cardinal Corripio Ahumada. The coffin holding Monsignor Romero's body was located on the cement steps between the altar and the iron bars which held back the crowd.

The multitude sang hymns from the Peasant Mass, the same ones they used to sing when Monsignor officiated at Sunday Mass and preached his popular homilies.

Members of the Boy Scouts and the Red Cross were in charge of keeping order at the main entrance and assisting the faithful who fainted under the intense sun or were overcome by the press of the crowd.

The long parade of the popular organizations entered the plaza. To the sound of applause and loud hurrahs, the leaders passed by in front of the iron bars of the entrance. One of them placed a wreath of flowers near the casket.

Suddenly, as Cardinal Corripio Ahumada was preaching his homily, a loud explosion was heard, frightening the already tense crowd. Immediately a clamor of general surprise was heard, which quickly turned into screams of terror.

Over the Cathedral's loudspeakers, a voice tried to calm the masses who now were running terrified in all directions, screaming desperately, in search of refuge. More shots were heard. Panic seized the multitude. Men, women, and children were trampled and disappeared beneath the crowd as it fled blindly.

I tried to remain calm, move to one side, and let the people run, but I was dragged along by a stampede of bodies that came upon me with such force that it made me fall on top of others who were already rolling on the ground. Miraculously, someone extended a hand to me and I was able to get up and run to avoid being trampled again. Elderly people and women with children in their arms dragged themselves along the pavement, trying uselessly to avoid the stampede. But there was no safe refuge.

The group I was part of crashed into the iron bars of the main entrance to the Cathedral. People were screaming, crying, and falling, sinking into the crowd.

We begged them to open the iron gate. The most desperate people were climbing on others and reaching up to scale the bars. Others offered their shoulders so that women and children could climb over the gate and run to take refuge inside the church.

There was a moment when I thought I would faint and be suffocated in that prison of pain-twisted faces. I feared that the strong pressure exerted by the crowd would crush me against the bars. Screams of terror mixed with the sounds of gunfire which could now be heard closer and louder.

Someone begged: "Protect Monsignor's body!"

The bishops decided to end the funeral with a quick ceremony.

Finally the iron gate of the main entrance was opened and the great mass of the faithful overflowed into the Cathedral, knocking over the wooden altar and trampling those who fell on the steps of the temple.

I tried to lift a woman who was lying on the cracked cement steps, but I was unable to move her. She appeared to have a dislocated foot and her face was covered with blood. Someone else came to help and we dragged her inside. She was groaning with pain from several wounds, the deepest of which could be seen on her thigh. A priest came over to comfort her at the same time he tried to calm the people in a language no one seemed to understand. "Something very vile is happening here, something very vile!" he said in English.

The words and gestures of the cleric revealed frustration and anger more than consolation.

Gerardo Barrios Plaza was strewn with papers and shoes. Dozens of wounded and trampled people lay unconscious on the hot cement of the park.

Several individuals had taken up positions in the park and were shooting at supposed snipers stationed in the buildings that formed the quadrangle of the plaza.

In the neighboring streets, vehicles burned and exploded. The noise reached the interior of the church, making the refugees fear that the temple itself would be invaded and converted into a battleground.

Everyone had lost something or someone. They cried out loudly for their children, spouses, uncles, aunts, brothers, and sisters. They implored God that those they were missing had not been trampled.

Minutes after the first bomb blast was heard, the solemn ceremony had turned into panic, stampede, pain and death. A real hell.

"What a way to honor Monsignor Romero," someone said. "As if the devil himself had planned this funeral of terror."

"They assassinated him in a cowardly way," commented another. "And they didn't even let us bury him in peace."

"That's because they fear Monsignor as much dead as alive," declared a woman.

The immediate problem of the refugees in the Cathedral was how to get home without endangering themselves. The shooting and explosions in the street and surrounding areas had died down, but the people feared being ambushed. The space within the church was completely full. Some people were beginning to suffer from lack of oxygen. There were wounded in urgent need of medical assistance.

The bishops decided that we could begin to leave slowly and silently, with our hands up to show that we would not cause anyone problems. And that is what we did. Slowly and hesitantly, each of us left by the route that was most convenient.

I faced the street a bit dazzled by the burning sun, suddenly aware of my physical appearance. I was missing one shoe. My white shirt was torn, revealing my arms, which were covered with bloody scratches. My pants were also torn up to the knees. In spite of all this, I considered myself fortunate to have survived the funeral.

But the nightmare did not end there. When I arrived at La Libertad Park, a block from the Cathedral, I saw that there was a battle going on. Several individuals had overturned cars to form barricades. They were shooting toward the building of the Coffee Growers' Corporation. I thought of taking another route to Barrio San Jacinto, but the bullets made me decide instead to return and take refuge in the Cathedral and remain there until the situation calmed down.

Many others made the same decision and returned to hide in the church. They swore they had seen tanks in the surrounding streets. Some of them claimed that individuals dressed in civilian clothes were riding in taxis throughout the city shooting at anyone dressed in black. They were saying that on Venezuela Boulevard there was a battle between government troops and guerrilla squads and that some masked men had stopped a taxi and taken out its passengers and killed them, shooting them in the throat because they were wearing bulletproof vests.

The terror had returned, violently shattering the supposed truce agreed upon for the funeral of Monsignor Romero.

People continued arriving at the Cathedral, lamenting the impossibility of returning to their homes. Many of them were peasants, who with great personal sacrifice had made the pilgrimage from remote towns to come bid farewell to their spiritual leader.

Early in the afternoon they closed the temple and we were forced to abandon our place of refuge. As I left, I said a last, secret goodbye to Monsignor Romero, whose body rested forever there in the church.

35 DEAD AND 450 WOUNDED REPORTED AT
MONSIGNOR ROMERO'S FUNERAL.

As I was closing the door of the boarding house to go to work, I heard Simón's voice: "Rogelio, don't go! You've got a phone call!"

His shouts surprised me, since I rarely received telephone calls, especially so early in the morning. Maybe it was Lourdes. I had not heard from her since the day I saw her at the market.

Simón, also a little surprised, handed me the phone.

"This is Domínguez. Pay close attention to what I'm going to tell you. Don't say anything. Don't go to the office today; do you understand? I'll meet you at the Oasis at 12:00. See you there."

Simón was still standing next to me. Seeing the worry on my face, he asked, "What's happening, Rogelio? Bad news?"

"I don't know. I wouldn't know what to tell you. The only thing I know is that I shouldn't go to work this morning."

"Damn! Don't tell me you're out of work again!"

"I don't have the faintest idea what this is all about."

I returned to my room, trying to convince myself that there was nothing to worry about. What I knew, for now, did not give me sufficient reason to worry. After all, it was just a short message. Maybe Domínguez got drunk last night. Probably he didn't go to work this morning because he had a hangover and wanted to have a drink with me to make himself feel better. It wouldn't be the first time.

I turned on the radio and, to calm my nervousness, began to retouch a drawing I had started a long time ago.

At twelve o'clock on the dot I was entering The Oasis Restaurant. The bartender pointed out the back table where Domínguez was.

The boss asked me to sit down and I could tell immediately that something was wrong. His face was drawn, more wrinkled than usual. Eyes wet and red. Hair uncombed. His white shirt rumpled, as if he had slept with his clothes on and had had a bad night.

"What's going on, Domínguez? Are you sick? It looks like the hangover really has you messed up."

"What hangover!" *The Tribune* has been bombed and destroyed! All the editors and I have been threatened with death. You, too."

"Me? Why me? I'm not involved in politics. I'm just a simple employee of *The Tribune*."

"You were," he said bitterly. "There's nothing left of *The Tribune* but rubble. *The Tribune* no longer exists, do you understand?"

When he uttered these last words, he began to cry. As if he had just been told that the person he loved most in the world had died.

"Incredible," was the only thing I was able to murmur.

Domínguez was crying, pounding the table with his fist, not caring that the other customers could hear him.

"No one could ever fully understand what *The Tribune* meant to me...it was my life... It was there that I was born, grew up, grew old. I considered myself useful to society there. My voice was on its pages. My conviction... And, though at times it was hidden among obscure words, there also was my protest against the system. My determination to cooperate in building a better world... Do you know that I knew that building from top to bottom? I began to identify so much with that big dark cement building that it was like my own body. Inside it my life thrived. Things seemed to have meaning... I was sure that the pages of *The Tribune* would end up just as often before the eyes of the poor as of the rich, of the government as of the rebels. That inspired me. Do you understand? *The Tribune's* pages were, to me, like a secret tunnel that connected me with the sentiments of the people, that permitted me to establish direct communication with the conscience of society... And that, the possibility of having a silent dialogue, in which I had the opportunity to filter a small hope of salvation to the hopeless, to offer a minimal ideal of human progress to the unfortunate, that was what kept me standing in the midst of the chaos... It was my boat floating on this sea of blood... But now, the storm has torn my boat to pieces... It has destroyed my very life..."

The boss was trembling with fury and helplessness. He was crying openly. The bartender came over to calm him and offered him a beer which Domínguez rejected. The man understood his pain and left.

"I feel like shit, Rogelio! I feel like shooting myself. I can't stand this sea of blood, pain, and disgust anymore. Of rotting cadavers. Of general destruction. Of people in rags killing their neighbors in order to survive... Say something to me, Rogelio! Don't just sit there! Convince me that, even though everything is collapsing around me, there is still hope, a way out, before I give up, too. Explain to me how I can get used to this constant, cruel masochism and sadism... At least smile at me, Rogelio, before I blow myself away right here..."

Domínguez put his hand to his belt, took out a pistol and put it on the table. I reacted quickly, grabbing a napkin and putting it on top of the weapon to cover it.

"Don't do it, Domínguez!" I said, trying to keep calm. "Don't do something crazy!"

I put my hand under the napkin and, ever so carefully, took the revolver from my boss's hand and put it in my pocket.

"Drink the beer, Domínguez; it will calm your nerves."

"I feel like I can't go on," he said after tipping the bottle and taking a swallow. "Even my childhood friend, Monsignor

Romero, was viciously assassinated. He who comforted us with his voice. He who kept our faith in the future alive... Help me, Rogelio! Can't you see that all I can do is cry like a helpless orphan... Never again will I hear that voice defying the darkness. Never again will I see him moving among the shadows, leaving light and hope in his path... Never again will his smile descend into the mud to anoint those who suffer, because perhaps the devil himself, embarrassed and resentful of Monsignor's nobility, dug his claws into him and made him return to the dust..."

The old man fell silent and put his head down on the table. He cried and blew his nose loudly. The restaurant was full of customers because it was lunch hour. But the voices, the loud laughter, and the impassioned song on the juke box did not seem to reach us, nor interfere with the grief of Domínguez, who gave the impression that he had deflated and that, from one moment to the next, he might sink under the table and collapse on the floor.

As I observed the old man consumed in his sadness, I struggled to put aside my own desperation and regain my calm. Suddenly I felt a sharp pain in my stomach, as if my old ulcers were threatening to return. After meditating awhile, I took one of the old man's hands and, squeezing it between mine, I said to him: "Domínguez, the best thing for you to do is to leave the country... Go to Costa Rica where your brother is...I'll go with you... This doesn't make any sense anymore. To stay here is to resign ourselves to die. Let's pack our bags tonight and we'll get the hell out of here tomorrow. Before it's too late."

BODIES OF EDITOR AND PHOTOGRAPHER OF
THE CHRONICLE ARE FOUND.

Blood
I see you being reborn
in the hands building the roads.

In the dark skin
of the one who now asks to be heard.

In the eyes
that no longer unearth the defeats
of the past.

Blood.

Stir

   circulate

     and

       burn.

Don't give in
    or fall
Because a young vein carries you.
Because a human vision renews you.

        Lourdes

Everything was ready for my departure. The taxi was waiting outside. I said goodbye to Simón and his family.

"Good luck, Rogelio," he said with a warm handshake, as if I were the one going to danger, and not they who were staying behind in the very center of the battlefield.

His wife couldn't say a word. She hugged me, her eyes full of tears, while the children watched the farewell with the dark eyes of their sad little faces. Holding out their dirty hands to me, they said goodbye with their sweet voices.

I had planned to leave at a time when the other tenants were not at home. I thought it best to tell no one of my departure except the owner. To do otherwise would only drag out this sad moment, when with some last-minute words and cordial gestures we put an end to a long sharing of joys and sorrows.

I would never forget this old house where I painted so many pictures. I laughed. I cried. I went hungry and felt disconsolate. And above all, where I met Lourdes. The being who honored me with her love, her joy of living, her poetry. Who made me understand the grandeur of this land where I was born, but that fate, bad luck, or perhaps cowardice, was forcing me to abandon.

I hurried out, with a lump in my throat. I threw my suitcase into the taxi, got in, and closed the door without looking back at the boarding house. I asked the driver to take me to the bus station. That was all I said during the trip.

The car travelled through neighborhoods, past ramshackle homes and shacks where people toasted by the burning sun milled. Half-naked children, pot-bellied and filthy, played, jumping over puddles of dirty water.

I was passing through this gloomy panamora one last time as if to relegate it to the past once and for all, but I understood very well that it would be difficult to erase the memory of the city's faces and grimaces. What will not remain etched in my mind are the mansions of the sumptuous neighborhoods, with clean avenues meticulously designed and constructed, adorned with flowers of many colors, cared for by servants and guarded by big, frightening pure-bred dogs. On the contrary, what will remain in my memory, perhaps forever, are the cardboard houses, the poor neighborhoods and rundown boarding houses with corners marked by piles of garbage, flies, rats, and the excrement of sick, nomadic dogs. Because those are the areas of the city where the heroes of existence walk. People who day and night confront irreversible poverty.

The taxi arrived at the bus station. I paid the driver and got out with the suitcase that easily held my few belongings. At that moment a protest march was going by, and I was unable to cross the street to catch the bus. I had to step to one side and wait.

The demonstrators were carrying colorful posters and banners: "THE PEOPLE DEMAND THEIR RIGHTS." "JOIN THE PEOPLE'S STRUGGLE." "MONSIGNOR ROMERO MARTYR OF EL SALVADOR."

"Rogelio, over here!" I heard Domínguez' voice and saw him sticking his head out of the window of the bus parked on the other side of the street.

I signalled to him to let him know that I was waiting for the protest march to go by, but it halted, leaving me in the midst of the demonstrators.

The woman who was leading the march was shouting through a megaphone: "JOIN THE STRUGGLE OF YOUR PEOPLE!"

And the crowd was responding: "THE PEOPLE WILL OVERCOME!"

Suddenly, two truckloads of soldiers appeared at one of the corners and, immediately, shots were heard. People began to run helter-skelter. Some fell to the ground wounded and were trampled in the confusion. Flags, banners and posters were strewn about by the demonstrators themselves and by the wind. Cries of pain were heard.

"Rogelio, don't stand there!" shouted Domínguez. "Hurry, so you don't get hurt!"

The voice over the megaphone was asking the demonstrators to throw themselves to the ground or seek refuge. People were falling wounded in the middle of the street, screaming curses of anger at the soldiers.

From among the thick crowd of demonstrators now came machine-gun fire and molotov cocktails that shook the trucks violently. Soldiers fell heavily to the pavement.

Faced with this intense counterattack, the soldiers tried to withdraw, but one of the trucks hit a light post. The pole fell on the vehicle and, under the rain of homemade bombs, the truck caught on fire, becoming a gigantic flame, until it finally exploded.

The other truck could not get away either. Its tires and engine had been destroyed by the persistent shooting of an individual who, entrenched behind some bodies in the middle of the street, was ordering his companions to withdraw while he kept the soldiers under fire. Two soldiers jumped down from the truck, enraged, and confronted him; they exchanged heavy fire. The soldiers fell. The other man also lay motionless in a pool of his own blood, his hands still gripping the machine gun.

I witnessed this violent scene from the ground where I had thrown myself down when the fighting started. I noticed that the man with the machine gun showed signs of life; he was struggling to take off the red handkerchief that covered his face. I got up and ran to him.

"Rogelio, get over here! Hurry!" I heard Domínguez shouting.

I reached the masked man and pulled off the handkerchief that seemed to be suffocating him. When I saw his face I could not hold back a cry of surprise. I fell on my knees next to him.

"Ignacio!" I exclaimed, gently taking his bloody head in my hands.

When he recognized me he forced a smile that immediately became a grimace of pain.

"I knew you were alive, Nacho!" I said in my emotion at seeing him again after so long. "Don't move; you're bleeding a lot... I've been looking for you for two years, ever since I came back from New York."

"Rogelio, my brother... I wanted to go beyond art...to paint the most beautiful picture...the freedom of the people... I know that you will...paint...make art...for both of us..."

Those were his last words. Ignacio's head fell against my chest. He was dead!

Sirens were heard and an ambulance arrived. Someone took the body from my arms, put it into a car and took off at great speed.

I remained standing in the street that was strewn with the wounded, the dead, and blood. I was still unable to believe that I had finally found my brother painter. I couldn't accept that I had seen him die in my arms.

The medical personnel were assisting the wounded and covering the dead with white sheets.

"We need volunteers to help us take care of all these people!" shouted one of them. "You, young man, help us! There are only two of us and there are so many victims."

"Let's go, Rogelio!" called Domínguez. "Come on, get in, let's go," he said, reaching to me through the window of the bus that now drove up for me. "Get in, get in, let's go," he begged, his hands now almost touching me.

"You go, Domínguez! You go; I'm staying!"

"You can't, Villaverde!" he stammered, incredulous. "If you stay, you'll die. Remember you've been threatened with death. Get in and let's get the hell out of here!"

"Go," I said firmly, looking him right in the eye. "Don't you see that these wounded people need me?"

The old man's face froze. He realized that finally I had decided something in an irrevocable way. As if it were the first important decision of my life. He frowned and his face grew somber for a few seconds, but then he smiled a strange smile.

I held out my hand to say goodbye, and he squeezed it warmly between both of his.

"Take care of yourself, Rogelio," he said tearfully. "Do it for this old man who grew to love you like a son."

"Someday we'll be together again," I said, my voice breaking. "If we're lucky enough to be alive when we wake up from this nightmare."

The bus drove away, leaving behind a thick trail of foul-smelling, black smoke. I stood there watching it go, its silhouette growing smaller and smaller until it became just a tiny dot that the distance swallowed up.

A white medical worker's jacket was thrown over my shoulders. I put it on and began to examine the bodies lying on the hot asphalt, hoping to find one that showed signs of life and rescue it from the jaws of death.

(October 1970–August 1989)

Monsignor Romero's homilies were excerpted from "La voz de los sin voz: La palabra viva de Monsignor Romero." (*The Voice of the Voiceless*: The living word of Monsignor Romero) 1980, UCA/Editores, El Salvador.

About the Author

Mario Bencastro, author and playwright, was born in Ahuachapán, El Salvador, in 1949.

The author's first novel, *A Shot in the Cathedral*, was chosen from among 204 works as a finalist in the "Novedades y Diana International Literary Prize 1989" in Mexico, and was published by Editorial Diana in January, 1990.

In 1994, Mario Bencastro's short novel *The Flight of the Lark* was chosen as a finalist in the "Felipe Trigo Literary Prize," Badajoz, Spain.

In 1988 he wrote and directed *Crossroad*, performed by the Hispanic Cultural Society Theater Group at Thomas Jefferson Theater in Arlington, Virginia in October of that year. This play was chosen for the "Bicentennial Festival for the Performing Arts" of Georgetown University in April of 1989.

Between 1979 and 1990, Mario Bencastro wrote the collection of short stories *The Tree of Life: Stories of Civil War*, which was published in El Salvador in 1993 by Clásicos Roxsil. Two of these stories, "Photographer of Death" and "Clown's Story," have been adapted for the stage. In addition, the latter was translated into English and included in the international anthologies *Where Angels Glide at Dawn* (HarperCollins, New York, 1990) and *Turning Points* (Nelson

Canada, Ontario, 1993). The former is included in *Texto y vida: historia de la literatura hispanoamericana* (Harcourt, Brace, Jovanovich, Texas, 1991) and *Vistas: voces del mundo hispánico* (Prentice Hall, New Jersey, 1995). "The River Goddess" was included in *3 x 5 Worlds Anthology: Salvadoran Short Stories 1962-1992* (UCA Editores, San Salvador, 1994). "The Garden of Gucumatz" was first published by *Hispanic Cultural Review* (George Mason University, Virginia, 1994).

About the Translator

Susan Giersbach Rascón is an attorney who from 1983 to 1989 worked representing Central American refugees, most of them Salvadoran, in their attempts to gain political asylum in the United States. Since 1990 she has taught Spanish at Lawrence University in Appleton, Wisconsin, where she created and taught a course entitled "Art and Social Responsibility: The Work of Mario Bencastro." She has also translated Mr. Bencastro's *The Tree of Life: Stories of Civil War*, a collection of short stories, forthcoming from Arte Público Press.